MURDER AT THE ST. REGIS

Chef Dani Rosetti Cozy Mystery Series - Book 1

BY

DIANNE HARMAN

Published by: Dianne Harman
www.dianneharman.com

Interior, cover design and website by
Vivek Rajan

ISBN: 9798670046404

CONTENTS

ACKNOWLEDGMENTS

I've been wanting to write a book about a chef who travels to different parts of the world to cook for Very Important People (and yes, to afford her services, they are also very wealthy) for a long time. I figured it would allow me to virtually travel to exotic places all around the world!

This new series and the protagonist featured in it began to come together when I received an email from a reader. She asked me if I would consider having a female character as the protagonist in a series who was not involved in a relationship, who was successful in her career, and who traveled extensively.

I wasn't sure if a character who was neither married nor in a serious relationship would appeal to my readers, so I asked them in my newsletter. I received hundreds of responses, the vast majority telling me that yes, they would love a series where a woman was not reliant on a man for her support or her happiness. And that's how the Chef Dani Rosetti Cozy Mystery Series came about.

This book, Murder at the St. Regis, is the first book in this new series. Chef Dani is front and center, but as so often happens when I'm writing, the characters begin to write the book for me, as if they were whispering in my ear. Arthur and Anna are products of those voices. I think you'll enjoy them, because I've come to really be fond of them!

To all of you who took the time to give me your opinion on this topic, thank you!

To the people who work so hard behind the scenes to bring my books to market, thank you!

To my children and grandchildren who always ask if they're interrupting my writing when they call or come by, thank you!

And to Tom, for the countless hours you spend spotting things that I've missed, thank you!

To all of you who took the time to give me your opinion on this topic, thank you!

To the people who work so hard behind the scenes to bring my books to market, thank you!

To my children and grandchildren who always ask if they're interrupting my writing when they call or come by, thank you!

And to Tom, for the countless hours you spend spotting things that I've missed, thank you!

Win FREE Paperbacks every week!

Go to www.dianneharman.com/freepaperback.html and get your FREE copies of Dianne's books and favorite recipes immediately by signing up for her newsletter.

PROLOGUE

"Dani, I have to tell you I'm pretty excited about this. If anyone had told me when I was flying fighter jets in the Marines that I'd end up as a bodyguard for a television chef, I would have said they were crazy," Arthur said as he and Dani sat at her kitchen table figuring out what they were going to serve at their upcoming catered dinner at the St. Regis Resort.

"And Arthur, that doesn't even include all the cooking classes you've taken, the private security firm you've started, and agreeing to be my sous-chef for my VIP Catering company."

"Yeah, I'm some kind of a weird package. Just glad that the guys I was in the Marines with can't see me now in this sous-chef outfit. The apron would be the final nail in my coffin," the burly ex-Marine with the square cut jaw and buzz haircut said with a grin.

"Arthur, I'm still confused about something."

"Shoot."

"I know you were a pilot in the Marines and that you were in it for twenty years, but how does that segue to becoming a bodyguard?" Dani asked, as she wrote down some ingredients that she thought she'd need for the upcoming event.

"Well, there are some things I really can't talk about, and that's one of them. Let's just say that the Army has the Green Berets and the Navy has the Seals. What the Marine Corps has isn't talked about."

Dani looked up from her list and said with raised eyebrows, "I assume you were in some special unit that qualified you to become, as I've heard the expression, "a lean, mean, killing machine."

"You can assume whatever you like, although the lean part probably wouldn't be accurate," Arthur said. "Let's leave it that I was able to adequately demonstrate to the television honchos that I would have no problem protecting you."

She nodded, thinking about their recent experience when a crazed fan had broken into the TV studio and run down the aisle waving a gun pointed in Dani's direction, but had been slammed to the floor by Arthur. Fortunately, when the gun went off, the bullet went high and harmlessly hit a wall behind Dani. She would never be able to thank him enough for saving her life.

"Dani, give me a real clear picture of what you want me to do on these VIP gigs. And I have to ask you something.

Am I going to be a sous-chef in name only, or are you going to give me a chance to really assist you and cook?"

"Arthur, you blew me over when you had me to dinner a couple of months ago. To be honest, I was going to hire a sous-chef who had some restaurant experience, and I was going to hire you as a bodyguard. I sincerely hope that I never need one again, but if I do, you're the one I want.

"However, when I got home after dinner that night, all I could think about was how good the food you'd prepared was, and what an excellent cook you've become. I knew, from all of our conversations over the years, how much you enjoy cooking. By the time I was ready for bed, I'd decided to ask you if you'd like the job as my sous-chef, and I haven't regretted it for a moment.

"You were with me for eight years at the television station, so you pretty much know my cooking routine and how I like things. I think having you become my sous-chef is a natural, but I'm sure some of the employees who work for you at your security business would think otherwise. Which reminds me, have you told any of them about this?"

Arthur seemed embarrassed and then said, "No. I can't think of too many things that are farther apart than being a sous-chef and a lean, mean, killing machine as you put it. Somehow, they don't belong in the same sentence. I just decided that the people who work for me in my security business are my employees, and if they find out that I'm a sous-chef, well, so what, even I'm entitled to have a hobby."

"Sounds fair to me, but I'm sure when we go to other

places and are met by the people who contracted with VIP Catering Services, they're going to wonder about my large, scary sous-chef."

"That's probably true, but once they taste what they hired us for, it will be forgotten."

"Agreed. Now to business. I sent out notices about the new business, along with a price list, to a huge list of contacts I've developed over the years." She held up a sheaf of papers. "Arthur, just from the responses I've already gotten, we're just about set for the next couple of years."

"Are they all pretty much in the California area?" he asked.

"No, and fortunately I know how much you like to travel. I've been asked to do VIP catering in Savannah, France, Greece, Italy, and probably twenty other places. I'm absolutely amazed, because my prices are exorbitant, and I have some special needs which must be met," she said.

"I'm not surprised at the response, Dani. You're practically a household name because of all your years on television, but what special needs have you asked for?"

"Let me preface this by saying that I don't have to work. You know that I inherited a lot when my parents died in the plane crash, and that, along with the money I earned while I was on television, leaves me free to do pretty much what I want.

"So I decided that if I was going to do this, I would only take the jobs that would allow me to travel to new and exciting places where I've always wanted to go. That was my number one criterion. Number two was that the client would provide a private plane for me, so I can take Kiku, my dog, with me wherever I go. Third is that luxurious accommodations will be provided for my sous-chef and me, and fourth is that I have complete control over the food that will be served, which means I decide what the menu will be, end of sentence."

"Quite frankly, Dani, I would think people would really balk at that last one."

"Yeah, I thought the same thing, but these people just want to say Dani Rosetti prepared it. They don't care that much about the menu. I'm sure you've read about the huge amounts of money some singers get paid to do a couple of songs for some sheikh in Dubai. Well, this is kind of the same thing. It's their egos being massaged by themselves because they can afford to hire me and fly me in for the event, thereby impressing their friends or colleagues."

"Okay, I get it," Arthur said. "Let me ask you something else. Why are you even bothering to do this? I mean, with your money you could charter a private plane and go to these places as a tourist. You don't have to work. We both know that."

"You're right, Arthur. But we both know how much I love to cook. Coming up with fancy foods for some of the wealthiest people in the world is also kind of an ego trip for me. Does any of that make sense?"

"Yes, I can understand that." He grinned. "Now let me ask you something else. What's going to happen when one of these multi-gazillionaires wants you to be available for a relationship that goes beyond cooking?"

She shook her head vigorously and said, "Not going to happen. Oh, I won't deny that there might be a little romance here and there, but that's it. I decided a long time ago I'm not the marrying type. I'm perfectly happy with my life, and I don't need someone to support me. Never wanted to be tied down by a husband, a kid, and a white picket fence. No, that's not going to happen."

"Good. Last question. Do you really think we'll have any type of security problems at these catering gigs?"

"I sincerely hope not. I want you to be able to concentrate on your cooking while we're doing them, but I'm also aware that I've made a lot of people jealous, and I'm sure some of them would like me to fall flat on my face. Goes with the turf. And I would imagine that most hosts for whom I'll be working will have their own security as well."

"Well, for what it's worth, I've got your back, as always, even if my hands are caked with butter or something like that," he said, laughing.

"Good to know. Now let's get down to business and go through this menu for the St. Regis event. It's first up, and I want to make sure everything is perfect for it."

"As long as no one tries to poison the guests, we'll be fine."

"Arthur, take that thought out of the universe," Dani said.

Arthur made a show of grabbing some air and stuffing it into his mouth. "See, no problem. It's out of the universe."

Sometimes it just isn't that easy to take things out of the universe once words have been spoken.

CHAPTER ONE

It was only two more days until Dani's first VIP catered dinner, and she could hardly believe, that for the first time, she was finally doing what she wanted to do, not what her parents had expected her to do, or what the producer of her celebrity chef television show, Dishing with Dani, told her to do.

It had been a long journey, and at age forty-four, although everyone thought she was only in her early thirties, she was ready for it. She poured herself a glass of wine and walked out to the wraparound porch of her large home in Santa Barbara that looked out at the Santa Ynez mountains.

This was her favorite time of year, Spring. A blanket of orange California poppies was the only thing that separated her from the mountain range. She took a sip of the very good Archery Summit Arcus Pinot Noir and remembered what she'd read long ago about cooking and wine. Whoever it was had said to never cook with a wine that you wouldn't serve to the most important person in your life.

It had become her mantra, and she knew she was probably overthinking its importance, but she was certain that the best wines she used in her cooking were a huge contribution to her cooking success.

While Dani liked to think that a premium wine was responsible for her success, what she never discussed with anyone was her absolute belief that she'd been born under a lucky star. It had just taken a while to let the star shine solely on her and now it was.

She thought back to the night she'd gotten the call from the Napa police telling her that the plane her parents were on had crashed outside of the city, and they were dead. They'd gone on to tell her that her brother, who had piloted the family plane, was in critical condition in a hospital in Napa.

Dani had been in her last year of law school at the University of California in Berkeley, and she'd immediately driven to Napa, which was one of the hardest things she'd ever had to do. She and her parents had been extremely close, and she couldn't believe they were gone. From what the police told her, her father, Luigi Rosetti, along with her mother, Chiara, had been flying home to Napa after they'd attended a winery owner's conference in Oregon.

The memories of that night are fuzzy, but some things, even after all these years, stand out. Having to identify her parents' bodies at the morgue. Winery owners from throughout the valley gathered at the winery tasting room for a Celebration of Life type of event. The doctor telling her that her brother, Bruno, had finally come out of a coma, and she could see him.

Even though much of that time was somewhat blurry, she'd never forget her talk with Bruno in the hospital. She knew that Bruno liked to sample the wines from her parents' vineyard, sometimes more than was good for him, or in this case, her parents. She knew her father had spoken with him several times about his excessive drinking.

She remembered exactly what Bruno had said the last time she ever talked to him, which was when she'd visited him in the hospital. "Dani, I'm so sorry, I really didn't think the wine I'd been drinking at the conference would be a problem for me. I drove to Napa from San Francisco, so I could fly them in the company plane to Oregon. Since I'm the president of my investment company, getting the time off wasn't a problem.

"At some point, everything got fuzzy, and the next thing I knew I was in the hospital here. I am so, so sorry. It was all my fault. They're dead because of me," he'd said, tears welling up in his eyes.

Dani had sat back and looked at him in disbelief. He'd just told her that the reason her parents died and the plane had crashed, was because he'd been drunk.

He continued, "Dani, can you ever forgive me? We need to work together and decide what to do about the winery and the vineyard. I don't want to give up my business in San Francisco, so we probably should sell everything, including the house, unless you want to take them over. I'm the executor of their estate. What do you want to do?"

She'd heard of people who said they were so angry they saw red. Now she believed it. The room turned red, Bruno turned red, and she felt like she was in a living hell, a red, living hell.

The next words she said to him she'd never regretted. "Bruno, I never want to see you again. For all intents and purposes my brother died when my parents died. Sell everything, send me a check, and never make any attempt to contact me. You not only lost your parents in the crash, but you lost your sister as well."

She stood up, walked out of his hospital room, got in her car, and drove back to Berkeley. The following morning, she packed up what she thought she'd need, called a taxi, and went to the San Francisco Airport to get a flight to Paris. Dani had told her roommate that she could use her car and anything else of hers while she was gone, which she thought would be a long time.

It had taken a few months, but eventually she'd been accepted into the Cordon Bleu Cooking School in Paris. She'd never wanted to be a lawyer. That was her father's dream for her. Being a chef was what she'd always wanted to do, and she was a natural. Eighteen months later she left Paris, having graduated at the top of her class from the difficult cooking school.

She spent the next few years working in the finest restaurants throughout the world. Bruno had sold everything that had belonged to her parents, including the winery and the vineyards, and had respected her wishes of not contacting her.

He'd worked through an attorney, who had her share of the proceeds from the sale of the estate assets deposited into a savings account for her. When she came back to the United States, she came back as a very wealthy woman.

She had the freedom and the money to go wherever she was offered a good job, which was rare for a chef. And that included Florence, Marseilles, Athens, and other foreign cities too numerous to mention, and some of which were a bit fuzzy in her memory. She was in Savannah, Georgia, working at the finest restaurant in town, when a large party of television executives came for dinner.

The owner of the restaurant had told her they had reserved a private room for their meeting, and that she was to cook the most gourmet meal she could come up with.

Dani had spent quite a bit of time coming up with the menu, and she'd prepared an unforgettable meal, as a number of them had said when they'd left that night. But the man who stayed after the others had left was the one responsible for a new phase in her life, and the one who made Dani a household name.

Robert Greenberg was the producer of five Emmy award winning cooking shows on television, and he'd been looking for a fresh face. What he didn't know when he sat down at the gourmet dinner was that not only was the dinner going to be superb, but that he'd fall in love with the female chef who had cooked it, one of the most beautiful, exotic women he'd ever seen.

At the end of the meal the man who'd arranged the dinner, a local Savannah television mogul, had asked one of the waiters to find out if the chef was available to come out of the kitchen, so they could thank her. When Dani walked out, she received a standing ovation from the television elite.

The moment Robert saw her, he knew she'd be perfect for the sophisticated upscale cooking show he'd been thinking about. He'd interviewed a number of chefs, but none of them had the exotic looks he wanted to be associated with the show.

With her jet-black hair, large brown almond-shaped eyes, and Mediterranean complexion, she was a beauty. He was pretty sure that beneath her chef's jacket, there was a figure to match.

He made arrangements for her to meet with him the following day, and that afternoon they raised a glass of Cristal champagne to each other, toasting the show that Dani was to begin shooting in two weeks, Dishing with Dani.

The show lasted for eight years, each of which resulted in an Emmy for her and the show. She became a household name, as well as earning incredible amounts of money from the show and for endorsing different food products. Her face was as easily recognized as that of the President of the Unites States

It all came crashing down one evening when she was live on camera. The studio audience and the audience at home saw a crazed woman running down the aisle of the large theater-like room where the show was being filmed, brandishing a gun. There was a collective scream as a large man was seen throwing his full weight against the woman and body slamming her to the floor, which caused her gun to go off, narrowly missing Dani, the bullet going high into a wall behind her.

Within seconds the man had subdued the women. The police came, took the woman away, and the man, Arthur Martinez, Dani's bodyguard, went over to her.

"Dani, it's over. She was just some crazed woman. You're okay. Honest." He stood next to her, protecting her from everyone who wanted to crowd around her and make sure she was all right.

A moment later Robert Greenberg ran over to Dani. "Dani, are you all right? I was watching the show in the other room. Oh, Dani, I can't believe this happened."

Robert was beside himself, because it was well known in the industry that he was madly in love with Dani, and she'd rebuffed every attempt of his to have any kind of a relationship other than that of producer and star.

"I'm fine, Bob, honest. Just some wacko, but I've made a decision."

"Why do I think I'm not going to like what I'm about to hear?" he asked.

"Probably because you've sensed on some level that this has been coming. This season is about finished, and for some reason, I haven't gotten around to signing the contract for the new season, even though I know it's due. I guess subconsciously I knew the time had come for me to move on, Bob."

"Dani, please, please don't make a decision just because some nut case decided she was jealous of you or whatever. I'll make sure there's even better security in the future. Please don't quit," he implored, his hand on her arm.

"Bob," Dani said, "it's nothing against you or the network. It's just time for me to leave. There are some other things I want to do, and I need to be a little freer to do them, not tied down to a strict filming schedule."

He looked at her and saw the resolute look on her face. He'd been her producer for eight years, and had come to know that Dani didn't play games the way so many stars did. When they said they were quitting, they generally wanted more money or more perks. Not Dani. When Dani said something, she meant it, and he knew her mind was made up.

Bob thought about all the attempts he'd made over the years to have the relationship between Dani and him develop into something more than that of producer and star. It hadn't. Dani was firm about not wanting to be involved in a committed relationship, end of story. He'd finally accepted it, but he knew he'd still be able to be with her at the studio. He lived for those moments, and now they'd be gone.

Over the next few months, he became despondent. He'd never thought Dani would leave the show, and recently he'd heard she had started a business called VIP Catering Service and traveling all over the world. He had no choice. He'd have to do something, because if he couldn't have her, he didn't want anyone else to have her.

CHAPTER TWO

When she'd finished her wine, she walked back inside and went into her study, wanting to look over her notes for the upcoming dinner at the St. Regis. When she was finished looking at them, she went into her large pantry and double-checked that all of the non-refrigerated items she'd bought earlier that day were ready to be transported to the St. Regis the day after tomorrow.

Then she went into the large walk-in refrigerator she'd had installed and holding her list in one hand, checked to make sure that the refrigerated items were ready to go to the St. Regis and that the steaks she'd taken out of the freezer earlier, were beginning to thaw. They were to be the main course wrapped in a puff pastry with mushrooms and a Madeira sauce. Everything looked like it was ready to go.

She'd deliberately had Arthur go with her today to help her when she bought the food for the St. Regis event, so she could be free tomorrow if there were any last-minute glitches. No matter how organized she was, things out of her control could happen, and she wanted to be prepared for them.

Dani closed the refrigerator door and heard her phone ring, not knowing that whoever was on the other end of the line would be the cause of her life to change forever. She walked over to the counter where she'd left her phone, picked it up, and said, "This is Dani Rosetti."

"Ms. Rosetti, you don't know me. My name is Carla Lucci, and I'm sorry, but I have some very bad news. Your brother, Bruno, died an hour ago from a massive heart attack."

Dani was quiet for several long moments, then she asked, "What is, was, your relationship to Bruno?"

"I am his daughter's nanny."

"His daughter? I didn't know he was married or that he even had a daughter, and why are you calling me and not his wife?"

"His wife, Sofia, died several years ago from cancer."

"I see. And his daughter?" Dani asked.

"She is here with me." Dani could hear Carla take a deep breath and then she continued, "Mr. Bruno always told me that if anything ever happened to him, you were to have custody of his daughter, your niece. He told me that you were estranged from him, but he knew you'd do the honorable thing and raise her. He also told me many times that she was his sole beneficiary, and that you were named as her trustee and the trustee of his estate."

Dani felt like the room was beginning to spin, and she

quickly sat down before she fell down. "Carla, I know nothing about this. Surely the girl's mother had relatives."

"No, there was no one. Her parents died, and she was an only child. You are Anna's only relative."

"I don't know what to say. How old is she?"

"She is ten and looking forward to meeting you. Ms. Rosetti, if you don't take her, she will have to go into foster care, and Mr. Bruno told me many times that you would take her if something happened to him. He always said that Anna could not go into foster care," Carla said.

"Carla, you're her nanny, why can't you raise her?"

"Ms. Rosetti, I have six children. My sister watches them during the day while I am here. I cannot take on another child. My husband would leave me. No, you are the child's aunt, and her only living relative."

Dani was quiet as she tried to absorb what she'd just been told. "But I don't even know where Anna and Bruno live. How would I make arrangements to get her?"

"I think Mr. Bruno knew something was going to happen to him. You know he liked his wine, and I think his heart attack may have had something to do with that. Anyway, he had his own plane and his own pilot. He told me once that after the accident with his parents, he couldn't fly a plane

"I have contacted Richard, his pilot, and he will fly Anna to Santa Barbara tomorrow morning. I am staying here at

Mr. Bruno's home with her tonight. They will be arriving about 10:00 in the morning. Can you meet them at the Santa Barbara airport?"

"I, uh, guess so. But Carla, I know nothing about children. This is completely unexpected," Dani said.

"Yes, I can see where it would be, but Mr. Bruno believed you would make a very good mother for Anna. I have contacted his attorney, and he will be calling you in the morning."

"Carla, I'm just stunned by this. I'll meet Anna and her pilot at the airport tomorrow at 10:00. I'm just going to have to take this one day at a time. What do I need to know about her? Having only one parent, I assume she was close to her father."

Carla sighed deeply and then said, "I suppose now that he's gone, it really doesn't matter, but Mr. Bruno had a drinking problem, a severe one. Anna talked to me several times about it, and she was worried about it, as all children would be, particularly when they only have one parent.

"She's seen him fall down drunk, and a lot of other things a child shouldn't have to see, so probably in one way or another, I think she may be relieved that she doesn't need to be worried about him anymore. Because of that, I think she's a little old for her age."

"I see," Dani said. "Is she worried about what's going to happen to her now?"

"I think she'd be a fool if she weren't, yet while some

bad things could be said about Mr. Bruno, he was a very good father, and he always told her what a wonderful, successful person you were. Even though the two of you were estranged, he read everything he could about you and shared it with Anna. I think she's really looking forward to meeting you."

"Well, I don't think I've ever been at such a loss for words or not known what to do next. I apologize for seeming like a complete fool."

"You don't have to, Ms. Rosetti. Anna will be easy to love and an addition to your life. Trust me. If I could adopt her, I would. Here's my telephone number. If something comes up and you need some help, please feel free to call me."

Dani jotted down the number and then said, "Well, I can see that I need to do some things to get ready for her. I don't know where to start first. Oh, is she alright around dogs? She's not allergic to them, is she?"

"I'm sure she would be fine around them, but Mr. Bruno wouldn't allow her to have one. He said he didn't need anything else to worry about. I've never seen her have a reaction to any of the dogs she's petted when we've been out on our walks. Why?"

"I have two. One is a chihuahua, and the other one is a pitbull-mastiff cross. I guess you could call them from the sublime to the ridiculous or something like that, size-wise," she said laughing almost hysterically. She was afraid if she didn't laugh, she'd start crying.

"I'll tell Anna and that will give her even more to look forward to," Carla said.

"School," Dani said. "What about school? What grade is she in?"

"She's in fifth grade. She goes to a private school, and school is out in two more weeks. She's a straight A student, so missing the last two weeks of school won't be a problem for her. I really need to go now. Like I said, call me if you need anything, otherwise, Anna will meet you tomorrow morning at the Sana Barbara airport."

"Thank you, Carla. I'm sure this is difficult for you, and I appreciate what you're doing."

"Not at all. I love her like a daughter, and so will you. Goodbye, Ms. Rosetti."

"Goodbye, Carla."

CHAPTER THREE

As soon as the call ended, Dani punched in Arthur's number.

"So, did we forget to buy something today?" he asked as he answered the phone.

"No, but my life has just completely changed," she said.

"Well, in a good way or a bad way?"

"I have no idea. I have never felt this discombobulated in my entire life. Here's what just happened." She related the conversation she'd had with Carla almost verbatim.

When she finished, Arthur was quiet for a few moments and then said, "Wow, just wow. Dani, I don't know what to say. This is just unbelievable."

"I know, and I don't have a lot of time to get ready for her. I am so glad you and I did everything for the St. Regis event today. There's only a couple of things I need to do tomorrow afternoon. My immediate worry is what to do with Anna while we're doing the dinner at the St. Regis."

"Okay, calm down and let's think this through. First of all, she's going to need a bedroom. I think you've got a couple of them that you use as guest rooms. I've never had kids, although I have two nieces, one of whom is Anna's age, and three nephews, but I think she'd be thrilled if she could decorate a room the way she wanted to.

"Next on your to-do list is to find a nanny, and I just might be able to help you there. One of my security guards mentioned to me that his sister was fed up with the winter weather in Chicago and just moved to Santa Barbara. She's living with his family, and he said it's a little tight.

"She worked as a nanny in Chicago, evidently for a couple of wealthy families, and thought she could find employment here based on her credentials. As soon as I get off the phone, I'll call him."

"Thanks, Arthur. That would be a huge help. I'm a little concerned about Killer and Kiku. Anna's never had a dog and while Kiku, as little as he is, won't be a problem, Killer might terrify her."

"Well, considering I insisted you get that huge pitbull-mastiff guy for your protections, I'd be a little disappointed if he didn't scare her at first. But you and I both know that under all that bluster, he's a pussycat. He won't be a problem."

"I mean, seriously, Arthur, what do I do now? Do I have to keep her for good? I didn't even know I had a niece until thirty minutes ago. And now that I do, I can't put her in foster care. I guess as wealthy as my brother was, and since she inherited everything, I could get a house and live-in nannies and all that stuff for her, but really, that's just kind of upscale foster care. I'd feel guilty the whole time."

"Well," Arthur said, "I never met your brother, but you told me about your last conversation with him. I'm sure it was one he never forgot, and I'd also have to say, he just delivered the ultimate gotcha' for it."

"Yeah, I've been kind of thinking the same thing. Arthur, I don't have a clue how I'm supposed to do this aunt thing. I mean, what do girls her age do? Never in a million years did I think I'd be in a position like this. What if she hates me? What if her father poisoned her mind against me? What if she hates it here?"

"Dani, you know the old saying, just take it one day at a time. That's all you can do for now. Would you like me to go to the airport with you tomorrow morning?"

"I'd love it. We'd planned on making some garnishments for the dinner tomorrow at my house. Why don't you come to my house, we'll pick Anna up, and then come back here and make them?"

"You're afraid of being alone with her, aren't you?" Arthur asked.

"Terrified."

"Okay," he sighed," but I have to tell you the only thing I have going for me in that area is that I'm from a large family."

"Makes you more qualified than me," Dani responded. "Anyway, why don't you come to my house at 9:15 in the morning, and we'll head out to the airport. I have no idea how much luggage she has, so we'll take my SUV."

"Good idea. Don't think your BMW convertible would work. Fun for driving along the ocean, but not so good when picking up the new phase in your life."

"You have such a way with words, Arthur. Maybe Carla will find some document from Bruno that supersede his trust and leaves everything, including Anna, to Carla."

"Might want to do some attitude adjustment this evening, Dani, and I'm not talking about it being red and from a bottle."

"Yeah, you're right. One last question. What does one wear to pick up a child they've never even heard of who will now be living with them?"

"Josie's there today, isn't she?" Arthur asked, referring to the housekeeper who worked for Dani three days a week.

"Yes, why?"

"As I recall, she has children. Ask her. Plus, she knows what's in your closet."

"Good idea. I'll do it now. See you in the morning."

CHAPTER FOUR

"Bruno Rosetti's residence. How may I help you?" Carla asked as she answered the phone.

"Carla, this is Lucia Esposito. May I please speak with Bruno?"

"Ms. Esposito, I'm sorry to have to be the one to tell you, but Mr. Rosetti died from a massive heart attack a few hours ago."

"Oh, no! That can't be. I talked to him earlier today. Tell me this is some kind of a horrible joke. Just stop this and let me talk to him," Lucia screamed into the phone.

"It is not a joke. It is the truth. I am so sorry," Carla said.

"What about Anna?"

"She is leaving in the morning for her aunt's home in Santa Barbara," Carla said.

"No, that can't be. Bruno and I were ready to announce

our engagement. He told me that I would be a perfect stepmother for Anna. Several times he said that if anything were ever to happen to him, that Anna was to come and live with me. I'll come right over and get her," Lucia said.

"No, Ms. Esposito. It is written in his trust that Anna is to go live with Ms. Rosetti. I am sorry if there was confusion."

And I'll bet I know why there was confusion, Carla thought. *Call it a couple of bottles of wine for both of them. Plus, Mr. Bruno told me that he was going to break up with Ms. Esposito, because Anna couldn't stand her.*

"Carla, was that Lucia?" Anna asked as she walked into the room a few minutes later.

"Yes, sweetheart. She did not know about your father. She's heartbroken and worried about you. She wanted to come over here and take you to her home, but your father was very clear that you were to go to your aunt's home, as we talked about earlier."

"No," Anna said tearfully. "I'd rather go to some aunt's house I don't know than go to Lucia's house. She was always real nice to me when Daddy was around, but when he wasn't, she said horrible things to me, like I should wear a girdle."

"A girdle. Oh Anna, I'm so sorry, but as skinny as she is, I'm not surprised. You are absolutely fine the way you are. You are beautiful. I hope you didn't let her words into your heart. Did you tell your father?"

"I tried, but you know how Daddy was. He was fine in the mornings, but he never remembered anything at night. The last time I said anything, he told me not to worry about it, because she wouldn't be around much longer. He said he was going to end their relationship."

"He mentioned the same thing to me, but I wonder if he mentioned it to Ms. Esposito?"

"I don't know. How did my aunt sound when you talked to her?" Anna asked.

"She was very surprised by everything, but she seemed very nice. Anna, I know it seems like everything in your life has changed, but I have a good feeling about her. I think you will be very happy with her, maybe even happier than you were here."

"I hope so. What if she doesn't like me?" the little girl asked as she looked up at Carla with a scared look on her face.

"Sweetheart, she probably won't like you, because she's going to love you. How could she not? Now promise me something."

"Okay."

"I want you to know that you can call me anytime about anything. You know my phone number. It can be a problem you're having or you just want to talk, but I think your life is going to be better than it has ever been. Now you need to go to bed and get a good night's sleep.

"You're all packed, and tomorrow is going to be a very exciting day for you. I want you to be well rested. Go upstairs, little one, and don't ever forget that I love you," Carla said with a catch in her throat as she kissed Anna good night for the last time.

*****

Lucia Esposito set the phone down, not believing what Carla had just told her. She'd talked to Bruno earlier in the day when she'd called him to tell him that she really needed to get a commitment on a date for their wedding. He'd said they'd talk about it at dinner tonight.

After she ended the call, she sat down and thought, *and to think his brat is going to go and live with her aunt. That means the kid probably inherited all of Bruno's money that was supposed to be mine when we got married. The aunt probably gets it to take care of Anna. If only we'd gotten married as he promised, and he'd died, it would all be mine.*

She paced back and forth in the large room that overlooked her flower garden, thinking of what she could do about the situation. For a moment Lucia considered forging a document that would show she and Bruno had secretly been married, and were going to have a large formal wedding for friends and family in a few months.

Then she considered whether she could forge a document wherein Bruno rescinded his trust and gave her his estate. She realized that probably wouldn't work, because she thought that kind of a document required two witnesses or a notary public or something legal.

The more she thought about forging the documents, the more she realized a good forensic signature specialist would probably find something that would indicate it wasn't really Bruno's signature, either on the wedding document or on the trust rescission.

I'm going about this wrong, she thought, *as an idea took place in her mind and began to grow. If I get rid of Dani Rosetti, Anna will have no place to go. Naturally the bereaved fiancée of her father would be the logical place for her to go.*

There is no one else. Then I'd become Anna's guardian and as her guardian, I would get control of the trust money needed to take care of her. And if some of that was diverted, who would ever know? Yes, all that needs to be done is for her aunt to have a very bad accident, a fatal accident, and that shouldn't be hard to do.

She walked over to her desk, sat down, and began to make plans to become Anna's guardian.

CHAPTER FIVE

"Well, your life may be upended at the moment, but you look spectacular. Was Josie able to help you?" Arthur asked as he walked into her house the following morning.

"Yes. I told her what had happened, and she thought it would be a good idea if I didn't dress in something glamorous or business-like. She thought a pair of jeans and a casual top would be best. She felt that wouldn't intimidate Anna and would probably make her feel at home."

"I think she was right. You look very approachable, and I like it that you pulled your hair back in a pony tail, kind of a soccer-mom look."

"A soccer mom," Dani said. "Never in my wildest dreams did I think anyone would ever refer to me as that."

"Look at it as another side of your personality, an undeveloped side. By the way, I was able to get in touch with the possible nanny, Briana O'Casey. I told her to call. Did she?"

"Yes, she's coming to the house at 1:00 today. I liked her when I talked to her, and if she works out, that would be wonderful. One of the reasons I bought this property was because it has a guest house on it. I don't know if you've even been in it. I've used it as a second office when I write my cookbooks. It would be perfect for a live-in. Do you know if she has a place to stay?" Dani asked.

"I'm assuming not, because her brother, the one who works for me, told me that he and his wife will be glad when she finds a job, because their house isn't all that big and with her there, nice as she is, it's gotten a lot smaller."

"I hope it works out. That would be a big relief. We better leave. I don't want to be late and start off on the wrong foot with her. Do you think she's as nervous as I am?" Dani asked as they walked outside and got in her car.

"I don't see how she could be anything but. Poor kid. Loses her mother to cancer. A few years later her father dies from a massive heart attack, and then she's shipped off to an aunt she's never met. Yeah, I'd be willing to bet she's nervous."

It was one of those beautiful late Spring days in Southern California when everyone who visits there wants to live there. Twenty minutes later Dani parked her SUV in the parking lot of the small airport. She turned the car engine off and turned towards Arthur.

"I don't think I was this nervous at my first television taping. Thanks for coming. I could never have done it by myself."

"Yes, you could, but it's not a problem. Let's go meet Anna."

They walked to the nearby general aviation terminal and stood in the small waiting room. A few minutes later a sleek jet landed at the far end of the runway and slowly made its way towards the terminal.

"Dani, if that's your brother's jet, that took some serious money to get. It's a Learjet 75 Liberty. Wow, I've only read about them. I've never seen one in person."

"How do you know that's what it is?" Dani asked.

"You forget that in my former life I was a Marine pilot. I keep up on what's happening in the aircraft industry. I'd love to fly that thing."

"I've never asked you, but are you still qualified to fly?"

"Yes. I do a biennial flight review every two years, so I stay qualified to fly. I have a couple of friends who have planes, and I often fly them. Plus, I've had a couple of clients who have had private planes I've flown, so yes, I'm totally qualified. Why do you ask?"

"Just a thought. Anna is inheriting everything, and I assume that means the plane. As her guardian and the trustee of her estate, I'm in charge of everything. At least that's what my brother's lawyer told me this morning. And that means the plane is under my control.

"I'm thinking I could keep it here in Santa Barbara, and we can use it when we travel to different VIP Catering

Services gigs. It looks pretty big, but would it be big enough for Killer, Kiku, Anna, you, and me?"

"In answer to your question, yes. It's got nine seats, so being big enough isn't a problem. The problem is Killer. Think about it, Dani. Some client meets us who's afraid of dogs and sees Killer. That dog scares the heck out of most people. We can't risk that. Killer will have to stay home."

"I hadn't thought of it that way, but you're probably right. Oh, look, Arthur," she said as she put her hand on his arm and gripped it tightly. "Look at the little girl getting off the plane. The pilot is walking her over here. Do I look okay?"

"Dani, you look fine. This is going to be great."

A moment later the door opened and the pilot and young girl walked into the waiting room. The pilot looked around and then walked over to Dani. "Hi, you must be Dani Rosetti. I recognize you from your television show. I'm Steve Norris, and this is Anna, your niece," he said motioning towards Anna who was holding his hand.

Dani and Anna looked at each other for a moment, and then Dani knelt down and said, "Welcome to Santa Barbara, Anna. I hope you're going to like it here. This is a man who works for me, Arthur. I thought he could help us with the luggage. Do you have much?"

"No," the young girl said. "Just some clothes and Chester."

"Chester," Dani said. "Is Chester still on the plane?"

"No, he's in my suitcase," Anna answered.

"Anna, this may be my first misstep of many, but is Chester a person or something else?"

Anna laughed, a clear tinkling laugh that couldn't help but make everyone who heard it smile. "No, Aunt Dani, Chester's my teddy bear."

Aunt Dani, Dani thought, *that actually sounds okay. This may go better than I thought.*

"Well, in that case, I think we better get your luggage. I'm sure Chester is tired of being in a suitcase. He's probably missed you," Dani said as Arthur and Steve left to get her luggage.

CHAPTER SIX

Dani punched in the number for the gate code, and the big steel gate slid to the left, allowing her to drive into her large fenced compound which included the main house, the guest house and a three-car garage attached to the house by a carport.

"Anna, those two dogs you see running to meet you are my dogs. The big one's name is Killer, and the small one is Kiku. Kiku will probably give you more kisses than you've ever had in your life, and even though the big one looks very scary, he's a big love.

"When we get out of the car, I want you to stand very still and let them sniff you. You'll probably see their tails start to wag. When that happens, put your hand out, palm down and let them sniff your hand. That will make them calm."

"Do you think they'll like me?" Anna asked in a tremulous voice. "What if the big one doesn't?"

"I can answer that, Anna," Arthur said. "I bought Killer

for your aunt several months ago. He's actually a trained guard dog, but that's only if there's a problem. The rest of the time he's like a little pony, however, I don't think you should try to ride him," Arthur said with a laugh.

"Come on. I'll stand next to you. He knows me and it will be fine, I promise."

Arthur got out on the passenger side of the SUV and then opened the door for Anna. He could see her take a deep breath, but she bravely stepped out of the SUV and stood next to him.

The two dogs went up to Anna and as Dani had predicted, sniffed her, tails madly wagging. She tentatively put her hand out and Killer first sniffed it, then licked it. Anna giggled with delight.

"He likes me, Aunt Dani, he likes me, and this little one is so cute. He's so small. Could I hold him?"

"Yes," Dani said. "Let me pick him up, and you can hold him while we get your luggage out of the back of my car."

She picked Kiku up and put him in Anna's outstretched arms. Kiku lifted his head and licked her cheek. "He likes me, too. Can they sleep with me?"

"Well, they usually sleep in my room, but if they'd like to sleep with you, that would be fine with me. What do you think, Arthur?" Dani said.

"I think I'd start with them in your room, Anna, and see

if they get up on the bed on their own and if you're okay with it, I'm sure it would be fine. Your bed is a big queen-size one, so there would be plenty of room for all of you."

"I think I'd like them on my bed. I've never had a pet before, and now I have two dogs. I'm sorry Daddy is gone, but at least I got two dogs."

Dani and Arthur looked at each other, Dani inwardly wondering what in the world someone said after that. The elephant was in the room, and she wasn't sure what to do about it. Fortunately, Arthur walked right past it.

"Well," Arthur said. "I bet you'd like to see your new room. Dani told me she's going to let you decorate it however you want. And she also told me if you don't like the furniture, she's going to let you pick out new furniture. Let's go inside."

Dani and Anna walked into the house while Arthur brought in the luggage. Anna's eyes took in everything. Dani took Anna on a tour of the house, ending up with her room.

"This is your room. It's pretty big, and if you'd like to have a television in it, I'll get one for you. This window overlooks the front of the house that faces the road and the far window back there looks out at the Santa Ynez Mountains, one of my favorite places.

"You'll be able to see the dogs out there and their doghouses. It can get hot here in the summertime, and I like them to have a place to be cool."

Anna started to giggle. "What's so funny, Anna?" Dani asked.

"The doghouses. The big one looks like it's a little cabin and the tiny one looks like a midget's house."

"I think you've pretty much summed up the dogs. Anyway, back to your room. You have your own bathroom, and it will stay pretty much as it is other than if you'd like it a different color.

"I have to cater a dinner, that's my business, with Arthur tomorrow night, but I thought in a few days we'd go shopping for whatever you think you need."

"Aunt Dani, my daddy told me you were a caterer. We used to watch your television show together. When I found out I was coming to live with you I watched a lot of your old shows on TV last night, so I'd be sure and recognize you today."

"And so you did. Do you like to cook?" Dani asked her.

"I don't know. Daddy had a cook, and she'd never let me in the kitchen, but I think I might."

"From now on, you are welcome to come into the kitchen whenever you want. I don't have a cook. I love to cook, and I do all of it. The only people who work for me, besides Arthur, who's my sous-chef, is a cleaning lady who comes three times a week and a gardener who comes once a week.

"When I spoke with Carla, she told me she was your

nanny, but she had children of her own, so I assume she didn't spend the night at your house," Dani said.

"No, whenever Daddy couldn't be there at night, Carla's sister would come over and stay with me. Sometimes she stayed overnight when Daddy had to be away," Anna said.

"The reason I'm asking is that a woman by the name of Briana will be here a little later. She's a nanny, and I thought it would be good to have someone here for you when I have to be gone from time to time. I have a guesthouse at the far side of the back yard, and I was thinking if you like her, she could live in it, and then you'd always have someone here with you."

"Okay. What's she like?"

"To be honest, I don't know. Arthur not only works for me, but he also has his own business, and she's the sister of one of his employees. We'll get to meet her together. Oh, here comes Arthur with your luggage. You should probably get Chester out of your suitcase and make sure he's comfortable."

"Okay. I'm going to put him in bed, because he's probably tired," Anna said.

"I'm sure it's been a long day for him. Have you had him for a long time?" Dani asked.

"Yes, Mommy gave him to me just before she got sick. He reminds me of her."

I will not cry, Dani thought. *I will not cry. This poor child. No one should lose their mother and their father at her age.*

At that moment, something snapped in Dani, and she resolved to be the best aunt she could possibly be. It wasn't Anna's fault her parents had died and she'd had to leave her home and everything she'd ever known. She vowed to do everything she could to make Anna's next few years happy, whatever it took.

CHAPTER SEVEN

"I'm sorry, Talia, you're an excellent cook, and you were a great sous-chef for Dani, but I just don't feel you can carry a show on your own. I'm really sorry," Bob Greenberg said.

"But Mr. Greenberg, I got letters all the time from viewers who felt I was as good as Dani. If you'll just give me a chance, I know I can make my own cooking show a success. Please," Talia pleaded.

"Again, I'm sorry, but the answer is no for the aforesaid reasons. Dani's show was the number one cooking show on television, and I can't have someone who is inexperienced take over that slot. I need someone who has a large following."

He stood up, indicating that the meeting was over. He walked Talia over to the door and as she left his office, he said, "Talia, I wish you the best. Please feel free to use my name if you need a reference."

"Thank you, Mr. Greenberg," she said, her face averted,

not wanting to give him the satisfaction of seeing her cry.

She didn't remember going down to the basement and getting in her car. She didn't remember driving out to the ocean. She didn't remember parking in Jocko's garage which he'd left open for her.

The first thing she remembered when she thought back to that day was the overwhelming jealousy she felt for Dani Rosetti. No, it was more than jealousy. It was absolute, sheer hatred. She'd done everything anyone had asked her to do. She'd been a brilliant sous-chef. Everyone said so. But it still wasn't enough. According to Robert Greenberg, which he'd said in so many words without actually saying it, was that she didn't have star power.

And if he was right, she'd never get her own television cooking show. She'd spend the rest of her life making sure that she had everything ready for the chef, the star of the show, who wouldn't be her. She thought the old adage about always a bridesmaid and never a bride was pretty right on in this case.

She walked into Jocko's house and found him lifting weights. "Hey lady, how did it go with Bobbie boy?" he asked as he set down the barbell, he was bench pressing and walked over to her.

He tilted her chin up and lightly kissed her. "I can see that it didn't go well. Want to tell me about it?"

She fell against his chest, sobbing. When she finally got control of herself, she related what had happened at the meeting and what Bob Greenberg had told her. "I could accept it if he said he'd already filled Dani's time slot with someone else, but no, he more or less just came out and said that I'd never make it on my own, and it hurts." She started sobbing uncontrollably again.

"I'm so sorry for you, Talia, but I do have some good news." He looked down at her expectantly.

She stepped back and said, "What?"

"I got the part," he said, his voice rising in excitement. "I'm the number two guy in a television show that everyone says will run for years. No one doubts that the public will love it. Talia, our money problems are over.

"We can get married, and you can start cooking for all the A-list people we'll be schmoozing with from now on. I'm sorry you didn't get your show, but you know that old saying about when one door closes another one opens. Well, it didn't just open. It pulled me in, and you with me. Think of it this way. This is the beginning of a new life for you."

"I'm really happy for you, Jocko. I just need some time to get through this. I'm hurt, because Dani always told me what a great job I did, and she led me to believe, no she almost said that she was sure I'd get her job. She probably knew I wouldn't, and she just said that to get a better performance out of me.

"This was my dream. And now my dream has been shattered. I hate her. I hate her with every fiber of my being, and I want her to suffer. I hope her new catering company falls flat on its face. I hope it's a big failure. I hope she dies."

Jocko looked long and hard at her. "Talia, you know I have some connections from my old life. If you're really serious about this, I can make it happen. If something happened to her, there wouldn't be any catering company."

"Are you serious?" she asked as they walked into the kitchen and he poured each of them a glass of wine.

"Deadly," he said. He lifted his glass up. "To our new life, my new program, and your problem being taken care of." They both took a sip of wine, and then he said, "I think I better buy some Cristal champagne. With my elevated status, I need to start acting the star part. Should be fun.

"Now, I need you to get me all the information on Dani that you can, like what the name of her new company is, where she lives, who works for her, everything. It will take a little time, but the people I know will make sure that your problem is taken care of.

"There are some things you don't need to know, but family is family, and I have a big family who loves to do things for me."

"You mean I really won't ever have to think how much I hate her again."

"That's exactly what I mean," Jocko said.

"Will you tell me what happens?" Talia asked.

"No, and I don't want to know either. It will simply be the end of your problems with Dani. Now join me in another toast," he said as he held his glass up again.

"To Dani, may she rest in peace."

CHAPTER EIGHT

"Anna, you have all afternoon to unpack, and now that Chester's comfortable, why don't you come downstairs with me, and you can help me fix lunch."

"Seriously?" Anna asked. "You know I've never done anything in the kitchen. What if I do something wrong?" she asked, her brown eyes big in her face.

"Well, my feeling is you can't do anything wrong. There's no right or wrong in my kitchen. Some things work and some things don't. As a chef, I've found that some of the things I thought were my biggest mistakes turned out to be the best things I've ever cooked."

"But I've never followed a recipe. I do know how to set the table and where all the silverware and glasses go, because Daddy thought I'd be around people who would know, and he didn't want me to ever be embarrassed."

"Sounds like he was a very good daddy," Dani said as they walked down the hall to the stairs.

"He was," Anna said. "But he got tired a lot of times during dinner. Sometimes he slept on the couch. I'd try to wake him up and help him to bed, but he was too big for me."

Oh wow, what this poor child has been through. Not too hard to read between the lines and figure out why Bruno was tired during dinner. Too much alcohol will definitely do that to you. I wonder how much Anna knows? Dani thought.

"Okay, Anna," she said when they walked into the kitchen. "I want to start this out slow, so I don't overwhelm you. I'd like you to set the table for the three of us, Arthur, you, and me. Here's where I keep what you'll need for setting it. We'll eat here at the table in the kitchen."

"Okay, and then can I help you cook?"

"Lunch is a pretty easy meal. I'm just going to make some meat loaf sandwiches and a bacon pasta salad to go with it. Tell you what. Arthur and I are going to make some garnishments this afternoon for the catering event we're going to do tomorrow. I'd really appreciate it if you could help us with those."

"Sure. I'd really like to do that," she said.

A moment later, she heard Anna say, "Killer, no. Killer, what are you doing with Chester?"

Dani dropped the sandwich she was fixing and ran into the pantry where Anna, Killer, and Chester were. She quickly assessed the situation. It looked like Killer had gotten Chester off of her bed, brought him downstairs, and dropped Chester next to Anna's feet. Killer was laying down next to her feet alongside Chester.

"Aunt Dani, do you think he was going to eat Chester?" she asked.

"No honey. I think he was afraid you'd left Chester up there in your room all alone, and he wanted to bring him to you, so Chester wouldn't be lonesome. Wasn't that a good thing for him to do?" she asked, petting Killer on the head.

"If you look near Killer's bed, he has a lot of stuffed animals that are his friends, and he always wants them near him. I think he was doing that for you."

"Oh, Killer, that's a good boy. Thank you. Aunt Dani, is it okay if I put Chester in that other chair? I won't set a place for him or anything, but maybe it will make Killer feel like I know he was doing a good thing."

"Certainly, that's a wonderful idea," Dani said, inwardly hoping that she'd been right about Killer and that he hadn't been planning on eating Chester out of jealousy. He assumed that all stuffed animals in the house were his, and he grudgingly allowed Kiku to play with a few, but not many.

*****

"That hit the spot, Dani," Arthur said as he finished the last bite of his sandwich. "Thanks. I forget how good meatloaf is in a sandwich. But what I really liked was the bacon pasta salad. We need to make that for an event."

"Glad you liked it, but I think it should be served at a more casual event, and I'm sure we'll have some of those. After Briana comes, we'll start in on the garnishes. I told Anna she could help us. Speaking of which, Anna, why don't you go upstairs and unpack? I'll call you down later to meet Briana and see what you think. I want your opinion because she would be your nanny."

"Seriously, I get to help decide who's going to be my nanny?"

"Absolutely. You're the one who will be spending time with her, so that only seems fair, doesn't it?" Dani said.

"I guess, it's just that Daddy always made all the decisions in the family. Whenever I said something, he told me that he knew better than I did."

Please give me the right words here, Dani thought. *I am really in some unchartered territory.*

"I guess everyone has their own way of doing things. I like to hear people's opinions, because I'm not always right." Dani said.

"Okay, but Daddy said he was always right," Anna said, as she took Chester from his seat on the chair and headed for the stairs, followed by Killer and Kiku.

When Anna had gone upstairs, Arthur turned to Dani and asked, "How are you doing?"

"Better than I thought I would do. Worse than I thought I would do. I mean I am flying strictly by the seat of my pants here. Sounds like my brother was not only an authoritarian, but consumed way too much on too many occasions."

"Dani, you know what your brother was. You never had any illusions about him after the plane crash, at least that's what you told me."

"No, I didn't, but then again, I never knew he had a child or that he'd even been married. I never met the woman who was my sister-in-law."

"Somehow, I have a feeling if she'd lived, Bruno might have been a different person. Anyway, I want to fly something by you," Arthur said.

"Shoot, we've got a couple of minutes until Briana gets here," Dani said.

"Okay, here goes, and if you're not thrilled with the idea, let me know." Arthur took a deep breath and resumed speaking. "You know about me and that a traditional family is simply not in my future. Funnily enough, I've always wanted a child, but given my lifestyle and my business, even adopting would be a longshot, and in the end, probably not fair to the child.

"Yes, but you also know I totally accept who you are, and you're my closest friend," Dani said.

"I know that, but here's the deal. I've fallen head over heels for Anna. I'd like to be able to be around her, you know, take her places, do the kinds of things a dad would do. If and when you get married, I'll step aside, but if you're okay with it, it's something I'd like to do."

"Oh, Arthur, that makes me so happy. Of course you can. But let me make something crystal clear. I've told you before that I'm very happy with being single. I'm not dead, and yes, I enjoy a fling now and then, but there will be no husband for me or a stepdad for her as long as she lives with me. I guess it will be the three of us, with you and me raising her, at least if she'll let us."

"It's crazy, but when I saw her at the airport, I thought that's exactly the little girl I would have liked to have had. And then I thought, well why not, and maybe I can help Dani, too," Arthur said.

"Done deal. I hear the buzzer from the intercom. Briana must be here. Do you want to sit in on the meeting, or go upstairs and see if Anna would like some help?" Dani asked.

"I'll go see if she needs some help."

CHAPTER NINE

"Hi, Briana. When the gate opens, just drive down to the parking area. I'll meet you on the porch."

A few minutes later Dani walked out of the house as a young woman with flaming red hair pulled back in a pony tail got out of her car. She turned towards Dani and said, "You must be Ms. Rosetti. I'm Briana."

"Please come in, Briana, and from now on, the name is Dani, not Ms. Rosetti. Oh, and the big dog is Killer and the little one is Kiku. They're part of the deal. Killer looks terrifying, but he's very friendly."

"Just as I was approaching your house, I saw someone, I couldn't tell if it was a man or a woman, put something in your mailbox. I stopped and took this box out of it. It looks like it's a box of candy. Since it's warm today, I didn't want whatever was in it to have a problem with the heat."

"Thanks, Briana, I'll put it in the kitchen and look at it later. Come into the family room and tell me about yourself."

"I just moved here from Chicago. After last winter I decided I could not go through another one like that. I worked for the Ellis family for the last two years and before that another family for a year. I have always lived in the house and taken care of the family's children or did whatever the family wanted me to do."

"But you're not a housekeeper, are you?" Dani asked.

"No, no. Often the families would want me to do things like go to the cleaners for them or the grocery store when the children were in school. Kind of a gofer, I guess you could say."

"And the children you looked after, were they boys or girls?"

"Both families had girls. In my first family, there were three, five, nine, and eleven. In my last family, there were two, eight and ten years old," Briana said.

"I'll be honest with you, Briana. Until yesterday evening, I never knew I even had a niece, much less that she would be coming to live with me. Obviously, I'm way out of my comfort zone. I need someone to help me "parent," Dani said, making quote marks with her fingers as she said the word, parent.

"I also need someone to be here for Anna when I have to be gone. I own a catering business, and I travel from time to time. There is a guesthouse in the back of the property where you can live. I'd like to use both families you worked for as references, so if you can provide me with those, I'll call them immediately."

Dani continued, "Assuming everything works out, which I have no doubt it will, I'd love for you to start immediately. I'll call the two families while you're here, and then I'll show you the guesthouse."

Briana had already prepared a resumé with the names and telephone numbers of references, the two families she'd worked for in Chicago at the top of the list.

Dani excused herself and went into her office to make the calls. A few minutes later she walked out and said, "Okay, if you're up for it, the job is yours, pending Anna's approval. Both families gave you glowing references. I'm willing to pay you $3,000 a month, plus I'll also provide you with your own living quarters, and you'll be eating most of your meals in my house. What do you think?"

"I think I'd like to meet Anna, hope she'll give me a thumbs up, and then see my new home. Assuming that goes okay, yes, I'd like to accept the job offer."

"Perfect," Dani said. "I'll go get Anna."

She returned a minute later with Anna and said "Anna, this is Briana. She's a nanny who would like to work for us, but before I officially hire her, I wanted you to meet her."

"Hi, Anna," Briana said. "What do you like to do? Television, reading, computer games? The girls I worked for in my last job were readers, and they read so fast, it seemed we were at the library every other day. For Christmas I gave them both subscriptions to Kindle Unlimited, so they could read as much as they wanted without having to go anywhere."

"I like some games on the computer, but I love to read too. I've never heard of Kindle Unlimited. What is it?"

Briana explained it to Anna and they talked about books Anna had read, what she'd studied in the private school she'd attended in Hillsborough, and the games she liked to play on the computer.

More adult than child, after several minutes, Anna turned to Dani and said, "I think you should hire Briana. I'd like her to be my nanny."

Dani grinned to herself at how very grown-up Anna sounded, and said, "Consider it done. I think I need to give both of you a tour of the guesthouse, because I imagine Anna will be spending a lot of time there. By the way, Briana, if I have to be gone overnight, I'd want you to sleep in my house. The guesthouse only has one bedroom."

As she stood up, Arthur walked down the stairs. "Briana, this is Arthur. I believe your brother works for him. Arthur, I just hired Briana. We're going over to the guesthouse, so she can see where she'll be living."

"I heard that as I was coming down the stairs. I think I'll start prepping some of the garnishments we're going to make this afternoon."

"We'll be back in a few minutes. You know where everything is," Dani said as she gestured for Anna and Briana to follow her. She didn't need to gesture for Killer and Kiku to follow her, since they automatically went everywhere she went, although for the last few hours, they'd been a little confused as to whether they should follow Dani or Anna.

They walked through the low-maintenance yard to the rear of the property where there was a small house matching the design of Dani's house with a red-tiled roof and cream stucco walls. Whoever had built the houses originally had the smaller house built very similarly to the large house.

"It hasn't been cleaned for a while, because it hasn't been in use, but I'll have Josie clean it tomorrow. It's not dirty, it just needs to be dusted and aired out. Maybe a light sweep with a sponge in the bathroom and the kitchen."

"This is great," Briana said. "I see there's room enough for a little garden behind it. Would you mind if I planted one? Chicago was so cold and windy that it was really hard to grow things there."

"No, the house and this area is yours to do with as you please. As you can see, it's fully furnished and towels and bed linens are in the hall closet. Other than fresh food, I think you'll find everything you'll need. During the day, you're welcome to eat at my house. Oh, and I forgot to mention that you can have Sundays off, unless I'm out of town."

"Thank you, and I love this little house. I'll go get my purse in the house, and then I'll leave to go to my brother's and gather up my belongings. I also think I need to go to the store and pick up a few things."

"You're welcome to what I have in the house, although I am catering a dinner party tomorrow night at an elegant hotel on the ocean, so maybe you should ask me first if you want to take anything," Dani said.

"I'm sure I'll be fine. Sitting out here on this porch with a glass of wine would be lovely in the evening when I'm finished working, so I think I'll pick up a bottle at the store," Briana said.

"Please don't. When I talked to my brother's lawyer yesterday, he told me that my brother was a wine connoisseur and had a large wine collection. He told me Steve, the pilot, would bring several cases with him on the plane when he brought it to Santa Barbara, and that he'd have the rest shipped to me. He said the wines were so valuable he really didn't want to leave them in an unoccupied house, and Steve did bring some with him this morning."

"Aunt Dani, what's going to happen to my dad's house and everything in it?" Anna asked.

"The lawyer and I talked about that as well. He's going to have Carla go through everything and pack up things he thinks I might be interested in. I guess he had several valuable paintings and some other artwork he suggested I take. I really don't need furniture or other household items, so I told him to have Carla hold an estate sale.

"I suggested he give her half of the proceeds. I really don't need the money, and anyway, she'll be doing all the work. Whatever is left will be donated to charities of Carla's choosing. The house will be sold, and the money from that will go into your trust fund, Anna."

"What's a trust fund?" she asked.

Dani explained it to her and that the monies in it would go for things like her schooling, clothes, etcetera.

"Can I buy Killer and Kiku some toys with it?" Anna asked.

Briana was standing behind Anna and grinned at Dani. "I think that could be arranged," Dani said.

As if either one of them have a clue how much money this child is going to inherit, Dani thought. *I just hope I can do a good job raising her, because that kind of money has ruined a lot of other people, and I don't want her to go down that path.*

I can't believe I'm even thinking that. Me, sounding like my mother did all those years ago, and I swore I'd never say things like that if I ever had a child. Well, at least I didn't verbalize them.

"Okay, let's go back to the house and help Uncle Arthur get ready for the dinner tomorrow night."

"Aunt Dani, you just called him Uncle Arthur, but he's not really my uncle, is he?" Anna asked.

"No, but he told me he'd like to pretend he's your uncle, so he can do all kinds of fun things with you. Would you like that?"

"Yes. This is a big day for me," she said as the three of them, plus the dogs, walked towards the house. "I got a nanny, an aunt, an uncle, and two dogs. And I get to help you get ready for a party."

CHAPTER TEN

"Okay, ladies, we each have a couple of carrots, zucchini, and potatoes for the vegetable balls. I decided we needed to do these first, since they take a little more time than the other garnishes," Arthur said.

"What do you want me to do?" Anna asked.

"I want you to take the melon baller, which is this thing," Arthur said, holding up his, "and push it in the vegetables as deep as you can. Roll it around until you make a ball, then put the ball in the glass bowl in front of you."

"I'd forgotten how pretty these are," Dani said. "With the little sprig of parsley, they'll look great on the plate next to the steak."

Anna stood up and said, "You said we could have the candy that Briana brought later. I think I'd like a piece of it now." She walked over to the box, opened it, took a piece of candy out of the box, and walked back to her chair. Before she could sit down, she stumbled and fell to the floor.

Arthur and Dani were next to her instantly, Arthur's hand on her pulse. "Briana, call 911, her pulse is getting weak. Tell them her pupils are dilated and her breathing is very shallow. She's unconscious. I think she's been poisoned."

"Briana, where did you get those candies?" Dani asked frantically. "That's all it could be."

"Like I told you, I saw someone put something in your mailbox that looked like a candy box. It was a hot day, so I got it out of your mailbox and brought it in when I met you. I put it over there on the kitchen counter. That's all I know about it."

They heard the sound of a siren approaching and Dani pushed the button for the gate. A moment later the kitchen was filled with paramedics. "I was notified that it's a suspected poisoning," the paramedic leaning over Anna said. "Tell me what you know about it."

Arthur told him exactly what happened. As he was talking, the paramedic administered a shot to Anna, who was put on a gurney. Two paramedics rushed her to the ambulance. "We're taking her to the Santa Barbara Cottage Hospital. Do one of you want to ride in the ambulance with her in case she regains consciousness?"

"I will," Dani said. "Arthur, take my car and follow us. Briana, stay here, and I'll call you when I know something."

"Dani, take these and give them to the doctor. Tell him

you need an analysis run on them immediately," Arthur said as he handed her the candy box. "Also tell him it smells like licorice, which is a poison commonly referred to as MCHM."

A moment later Dani was climbing in the back of the ambulance. She sat by Anna, her hand on Anna's arm for comfort, as the ambulance raced to the hospital. Anna's condition never changed during the trip.

They were met at the emergency room curb by two nurses who hurriedly wheeled Anna into the emergency room and down a hall after the paramedics had put her on a gurney. Dani ran behind the gurney. They rolled it into a room where a doctor was waiting to examine her.

He nodded to Dani and he and another doctor, who Dani assumed was his assistant, began to assess Anna's vitals. He asked Dani what had happened and she told them, then handed the box of candy to the doctor.

"Take this to the lab, stat," he said to a nurse. "I want a test run on these candies immediately. I'm pretty sure it's MCHM, so have the lab specifically test for that. The antidote the EMT gave her would be appropriate for that type of poison," he said.

After he'd examined Anna, he turned to Dani and said, "I assume that you're her mother. I think she's going to be fine. Fortunately, the antidote was administered within the very short window most poisons give us. This poison, at least the poison I think she ingested, has a very favorable rate of complete healing with that antidote. Is she allergic to anything?"

"Doctor, I have no idea. I'm her aunt. Here's situation," Dani said and explained what had happened to Anna's father and that now she was the child's guardian.

"I see. When you get her medical records, I'd like to see them. I'm a pediatrician and quite familiar with poisonings and children. I'm not seeing any signs of an allergic reaction, so that's a good thing," he said.

"What happens now?" Dani asked as Arthur ran into the room. Dani introduced them.

"I want to see what the lab test shows for the poison. If it's what I suspect, and based on what my examination shows, once she wakes up, I want to continue to monitor her for a few hours. If everything is okay, I would say she should be able to go home tonight. Oh, look, she's showing signs of waking up. That's good."

"Anna, Arthur and I are here, and you're going to be fine. The doctor wants you to stay here for a couple of hours to see how you're doing, and I'll be with you. How do you feel?"

"I feel very tired, and my mouth tastes like I ate licorice, but we didn't have any at lunch," Anna said.

"No, honey, we didn't. We think it was in the bite of candy you ate."

"I've never had licorice in a chocolate candy piece before," Anna said.

"And you never will again," Arthur said. "Anna, why

don't you go back to sleep for a little while? You've been through a lot. I have to leave for a little while, but I'll come back here to take you and Dani home."

He lightly touched her cheek and motioned for the doctor to follow him out the hall. "Doctor, I own a security firm and have been Ms. Rosetti's bodyguard for a long time."

"Of course, now I recognize her. My wife never missed her television show. I'm glad you said her last name, because from the moment I saw her, I've been trying to place her."

"I'm pretty sure the candy was meant for Dani. No one other than Anna's nanny in Hillsborough knows that Anna has come to live with Dani. That means someone wants to kill Dani, and I have to not only find out who, I have to make sure her home and the area around it are an absolute fortress."

"Yes, I think you should go and do that. From what I see on television, if a murderer is unsuccessful, they usually will try again. Am I right?"

"Unfortunately, yes. Here's my card. I'd appreciate it you'd give me a call when you get the lab report."

"Certainly, Mr. Martinez."

Arthur walked back in the room and said, "Dani, I'm leaving now. Give me a call when you want me to pick you and Anna up. I want to make sure the house and property are secure. I called Briana and told her to stay in the house until I got back. Naturally, I gave her instructions to not let anyone on the property."

She motioned for him to go back out in the hall and followed him. "Arthur, obviously those candies were not meant for Anna, but for me. Does this mean someone wants to kill me?" Dani asked shakily.

"Dani, I wish I could lie to you, but I think the answer is yes. I'll be staying in your house until we find out who did this and what it's all about. I promise you that your safety and that of Anna are my top priority. I will also have a couple of my men patrolling and guarding the property. You both will be safe."

"Arthur, the attempt on my life when I was filming the show several months ago was bad enough. But this is far more terrifying. Someone planned this. It wasn't just a crazed fan with a gun. Someone actually had to make the candies with poison or else insert it into the candy with a syringe.

"In either case, I'm scared to death. And to think Anna was poisoned on her first day with me. The poor kid. I wonder if I need to get a child psychologist for her. What do you think?"

"Dani, let's just take this one step at a time. Anna will know that you're here with her. I'll have Briana do the prep work we were going to do in the kitchen. We still have that dinner to take care of tomorrow.

"I've decided I'm going to have one of my men stay in the house with Briana and Anna tomorrow. They'll be safe there and I'll be with you. Do you have any thoughts as to who would want you dead?"

"Nice phrase, Arthur," Dani said with a grimace. "No, I mean I'm sure there are people who don't like me or are jealous of me, but enough to try and murder me. No, I can't think of anyone."

"Well I want you to start thinking about it, because I need to find out who did it, and trust me, I will," Arthur said with a resolute look on his face. "See you later."

CHAPTER ELEVEN

"Anna, how do you feel?" Dani asked her as she settled the little girl in bed for the night, both dogs lying next to the bed, sensing something had happened to their new friend.

"I'm okay. Can I ask you something?"

"Of course, sweetheart. What is it?"

"The nurse in the hospital told me I got sick because of poison in the candy. Is that true?"

"Yes, unfortunately it is."

Dani knew what was coming next, and she'd been trying all afternoon to come up with an answer that was true, but wouldn't frighten Anna. The last thing the child needed was to have another parental figure die.

"Why would someone want to poison me?"

"Anna, I don't think they meant it for you. I think it was meant for me. Evidently someone doesn't like me, or rather

I should say, hates me. I wish I knew who it was and why."

"Do you think it was the person in the grey car?"

At that moment, Arthur walked in the room to see how she was doing and heard her. "Anna, what grey car?"

"Aunt Dani, remember how after lunch you were getting ready to meet Briana and you sent me upstairs to unpack?"

"Yes."

"And then a few minutes later Uncle Arthur came up to help me."

"Yes, I remember, why?"

"I was getting my clothes out of my suitcase, and I kept walking past the window over there, the one that looks out at the road in front of your house. There was a grey car that kept going back and forth in front of the house. There's not much traffic on that road, so that's why I remember it."

"Anna, this could be very important. Can you tell me anything else that you remember about the car? Did you see who was driving?"

Anna was quiet for several moments, clearly trying to think if there was anything she'd noticed about the car. Finally, she said, "I can see it in my mind. It had a white line on the side and there were two people in the front seat of the car."

"This is very important, Anna. Were they men or

women or one of each?" Arthur asked.

"I couldn't tell. I could just see forms. And I tried, but I couldn't read the whole license plate."

"Anna, are you telling me you saw the license plate?" Arthur asked, his heart fluttering.

"Yes, it was a California plate. I can remember the last five letters and numbers. My teachers always told me I had an almost photographic memory."

"Wonderful. What were they?"

"A73Y2."

"Okay, Anna, that's great. Can you remember the color of the license plate?"

"Yes, it was black and the letters and numbers were in yellow. I remember Daddy telling me once that California had brought that type of license plate back from years ago, so I don't know whether it was an original license plate or a newer one."

"Honey, that's good enough. I'll be back in a few minutes. I need to make some calls," Arthur said.

A half hour later he walked down the hall to Anna's room and saw that Dani was just leaving. He peeked in and noticed that a night light was on in the room and the two dogs were sleeping next to Anna's bed.

"Dani, it's been a grueling day, but I need to talk to you.

Let's go down to the kitchen and have a glass of wine. Okay?"

"Yes, but let's make it a short night. I want to be on my game for the dinner tomorrow night. Thank heavens all of this happened today and not tomorrow."

Arthur took a bottle of wine out of one of the boxes that had been on the plane and opened it. He handed Dani a glass and said, "Like I told you. We need to talk. First of all, I had three of my men come out here this afternoon while you were at the hospital and they have made sure that your property is totally secured."

"Didn't you do that after the crazy gun woman incident?"

"Yes, but I wanted them to double check that there weren't any breaches in the system. I also wanted them to secure the guesthouse. Short of someone throwing a bomb at the house, no one and nothing can get on your property."

"I'm glad to hear that. I never saw Briana tonight. Did you take care of her?"

"Yes, she brought her personal things from her brother's home as well as some groceries she picked up. I also have you both on an app that is a walkie-talkie in case there's some problem with your I-Phones and you need to talk to each other.

"Dani, we need to try and figure out who is behind this. I don't think the candy was an isolated thing. When whoever is behind it figures out that you're alive, I'm sure they will make another attempt. I have you as well guarded as anyone can be, but I want you to think hard about who it is. Ideas? Who doesn't like you?"

Dani was quiet for several moments as she sipped her wine. "Believe me, Arthur, I've been racking my brain and I have a couple of thoughts, but nothing solid."

"Shoot. I'm all ears."

"Well, I've never met a woman named Lucia Esposito, but evidently she and my brother were an item. Carla, Anna's nanny, called me back last night to tell me about her, and how she had insisted that Anna be sent to her, rather than to me."

"Why would she do that?" Arthur asked.

"Carla thinks that Lucia is a gold digger. She told me that my brother had mentioned to her several times that all Lucia was interested in was his money, even though she pretended she adored Anna. Carla thinks she was hoping that she could be declared Anna's guardian, take over Anna's inheritance, and then fritter it away."

"All right. That's a person who could have a motive, but off the top of my head it seems that since she only found out last night, it would be very difficult for her to locate you and make the poison candy.

"Plus, she would have had to drive or fly here from the San Francisco area. I don't think I'll put her too high up on the suspect list. Who's next? What about that guy who was your producer? There was a lot of talk around the studio that he was in love with you."

"You're talking about Robert Greenberg. Yes, I think he was in love with me. At least he told me that on a number of occasions and wanted to have a relationship with me, which I always said no to. He seemed really broken up when I told him I was leaving the show, but I doubt that he'd ever do something like that."

"He's definitely going on the list. Unrequited love can be a powerful motive. And let's face it, he knows where you live, he knows what you look like, and he lives in Los Angeles, only a two-hour drive from here. I'd put him pretty high up on the list. Anyone else?"

"I'm sure my show's popularity made a lot of the other celebrity chefs jealous, but I really can't see any of them trying to kill me. I mean, they have television shows and they have fans, and for them to be involved in my murder would certainly ruin all of that for them. Celebrity chefs have egos and the fans and the shows feed those egos. I can't see them jeopardizing their status because they're jealous of me."

"Okay," Arthur said. "What about the people who were on your show? I knew a couple of them, but was anyone jealous of you there? I'm sure people were disappointed when you quit the show, but disappointed enough to murder you? After all, I'm sure your decision to cancel the show affected a lot of their income sources."

Dani was quiet for several moments and then she said, "There was someone who was and wasn't upset about it.

That was my sous-chef on the show, Talia.

"Bob Greenberg called to tell me that Talia had come to his office and asked to have her own show. She said that she'd worked for me for a long time, and she was sure she could pull in my viewers.

"He told her he didn't think she could carry her own show. Bob wanted me to know because she was quite angry about it, and since we were still filming my show, he wanted to give me a head's up that she might present a problem."

"And did she?" Arthur asked.

"Not really. I could tell she was angry and hurt, but she was also very professional about it."

"Dani, I have a feeling you're not telling me all of it. What else is there?"

"I'm sure it's nothing, but there were a lot of rumors about her boyfriend, and I understand that they either are or will soon be married."

"What about him?"

"Arthur, it's really just gossip, and I don't like to do that. Forget I said anything."

"Not when your life is in danger. Tell me the gossip."

"Remember the other night when we were watching that new show on television? The one with the two male leads?"

"Yes, what about it?"

"Well, the guy with the dark hair is Jocko, the husband or husband-to-be of Talia."

"I'm still not getting the whole picture. Fill in the blanks for me."

She took a deep breath and the said, "I don't think you're going to like this."

"I don't think I've liked what I've seen in the last twenty-four hours. Tell me more of what I'm not going to like."

"There was talk that Jocko was from a Mafia family," she said, quickly picking up her glass and taking a sip of wine.

"A Mafia family. That's swell. Did you ever meet him?"

"Yes," Dani said. "He was very nice."

"So he knows what you look like."

"Of course, but think about it, Arthur, a lot of people know what I look like. All they had to do was watch the show once, and there I was. Plus, I was on that show for eight years. Probably most people who watch daytime television saw me, even if they were only changing the channels. And don't forget my cookbooks. My picture's on the backs of all of those, so anyone who's been in a bookstore might know what I look like."

"That's true. Do you know Jocko's last name?"

"Give me a minute. It was an Italian name. I have a picture of a cheese wheel in my mind." She clicked her fingers. "Got it. Lucchese, his name was Jocko Lucchese."

"This is just great," he said sarcastically. "That's a very well-known Mafia last name."

"Yeah, when Talia introduced us, I thought that name sounded familiar," Dani said. "Arthur, that's it. I don't have any more names. And who knows? It very well could have been from a crazed fan who found out where I live, and we won't have any more problems."

"I like your optimism, Dani, but I prefer to be totally prepared. I'll check out the three people you gave me, and see what I come up with. And I do think it's time for us to go to bed. It's been an emotionally draining day, and tomorrow will probably be another one. Sleep well.

"I don't anticipate any problems tonight, mainly because whoever did this probably doesn't know that you're okay, but the house is being monitored just in case. My name is on that walkie-talkie app as well, just hit my name if you need me for any reason."

"Will do. I'm going to check on Anna, and then I'm going to bed. See you in the morning."

"While you're doing that, I'll do a walk-through of the house and make sure everything is okay."

"Arthur, thanks for everything. I don't know what I would have done without you today."

"Yeah, it's kind of weird to think I found a little girl I fell in love with and then almost lost her. All in a couple of hours. Couldn't have scripted that. Good night."

CHAPTER TWELVE

"Robert Greenberg's office, how may I direct your call?" the perky secretary said the following morning.

"My name is Harold Sharp, and I talked to Mr. Greenberg a couple of days ago regarding an idea for a show. He was going to call me back after he'd thought about it, but I haven't heard from him," Arthur said.

"Did you talk to him in person or on the phone?" she asked. "Mr. Greenberg is in New York and therefore, hasn't been in the office all week. As a matter of fact, he won't be in next week, either, because he and his fiancée are going to Italy for a little vacation."

"Well, in that case, it must have been last week. When did he leave?" Arthur asked.

"At noon, last Friday. You must have talked to him last week. I'll be speaking with him later today. Would you like me to give him a message for you?"

"No, that's fine. I'll give him a call next week. Thanks."

"Not a problem, sir. Have a nice day."

"And you, too."

Well, one down, Arthur thought. *Sure, Greenberg could have arranged for someone else to do the candies, but since he's engaged, rather doubt he's spending much time these days thinking about how he can kill Dani. He just went to the bottom of the list.*

*****

"May I speak with Carla?" Arthur asked.

"This is she speaking. Who is this?"

"My name is Arthur Martinez. I'm a friend of Dani Rosetti's, actually her sous-chef and her bodyguard. We had a little incident last night, and I need your help."

"Is Anna okay? What was the incident, Mr. Martinez?"

Arthur told her what had happened with the candy, the trip to the hospital, and how he had secured the property. He went on to assure her that when he was not personally with Anna, one of his men and a nanny would be, as well as two dogs, one of which was a trained guard dog and already devoted to Anna.

"Oh, no, my little Anna! Are you sure she is all right? Should I fly down there?"

"No ma'am. I talked to her this morning at breakfast, and she appears to be fine. The doctor who admitted her to emergency was a pediatrician, and he would not have released her if he had any doubts. Plus, he knew who Dani was, and he was probably afraid of getting sued if he did," he said with a laugh.

"Dani told him that she would be receiving a court order soon declaring her to be Anna's guardian, so she can easily get medical care for her, but since last night was an emergency, that wasn't an issue."

"Bruno's lawyer called me this morning about clearing out the house. I think it will take me a week or so." Carla was quiet for a moment, then she asked, "Do you or the police have any idea who did it?"

"No," Arthur said. "Actually, the police weren't called. I own a security company, and my men secured the house and the grounds. We didn't call the police, because quite frankly I was afraid of the publicity and didn't think Anna needed anything more right now. Dani's a well-known television celebrity chef, and I didn't want it to be in the papers for a couple of reasons.

"First of all, I didn't want the press to be harassing her or Anna. I was afraid they might use some zoom lenses or something and get a photo of her which I definitely do not want. Secondly, I was hoping to buy a little time and that the person who was responsible for doing it wouldn't know that Dani wasn't the one who had ingested the candy."

"I think that was very smart, Mr. Martinez. What can I do for you?"

"I understand that Anna's father was seeing a woman named Lucia Esposito. I also understand that you called

Dani last night concerned after the woman phoned you and wanted to take Anna."

"Yes, Mr. Martinez…"

"Please, not Mr. Martinez. My name is Arthur."

"Yes, Arthur. She wanted to have Anna live with her. She said that she and Bruno were going to be married and Anna would have been her stepdaughter, so she should have her, not some aunt she'd never seen."

"And I understand that Anna did not care for her, is that true?"

"Yes. Anna never wanted anything to do with her. She told me that when her father was around, Lucia was very loving and sweet towards her, but as soon as he left, she was mean and made fun of her."

"Why do you think she wanted Anna?" Arthur asked.

"This is gossip, and I don't really like to gossip, but given what you've told me, you should know. The woman who cleans her house is my sister-in-law. She told me that she's seen a lot of bills on Lucia's desk that are marked past due and several times she's answered the phone and the calls were from bill collectors.

"I think she wanted Anna to live with her so she could be declared her guardian and have access to her money. She certainly never seemed to care much about Anna when her father was alive," Carla said.

"Do you have any way of finding out where Lucia was last night?"

Carla was quiet for several moments and then she said, "I can call my sister-in-law. She doesn't live there, but she might know something. Would you like me to do that?"

"Yes, please. Here's my telephone number, and I hate to ask this, but the sooner you could do it, the better."

"I'll call her right now, but she may be working and not pick up the call," Carla said.

"I understand, and thank you for the information."

"Mr. Martinez? I mean Arthur, please tell Anna how much I love her and miss her. She was a ray of sunshine in this house, and it's very empty without her."

"I'll be sure and tell her," he assured her.

Arthur looked at his watch. *Okay*, he thought, *that takes care of two of Dani's people. I need to call my office and get them started on the third.*

*****

"Martinez Security, how may I direct your call," the voice on the other end of the line said.

"Hi, Lisa, it's Arthur. Is Jake in?"

"Yes, would you like me to put you through to him?"

"Please."

A moment later a deep voice said, "Hey, Arthur, understand there was a little excitement yesterday. Heard about it from the guys today."

"Yes, and it could have been a lot more than a little excitement. A few minutes more, and it would have been fatal."

"So I heard, but I understand the good news is that the little girl is well and doing fine now."

"Yes, thank heavens. I've got a few things I need you to do that take precedence over everything else. I'm trying to find out who was behind it and find them before they try again, which they will probably do when they find out Dani is alive and well."

"Shoot."

"First of all, I want you to get all the information you can on a man named Jocko Lucchese. He's in a new television show. Probably has ties to the Mafia. I want to know all about him."

"Got it," Jake said. "Next."

"Next is everything you can find out about his girlfriend or wife, a woman by the name of Talia Myers. She was Dani's sous-chef on Dani's television show."

"That shouldn't be too hard. Got any more?"

"Yes. I saved the hardest for last. A grey car was seen several times on the road in front of Dani's house just prior to the candy incident. Have no idea what the make, year, or model is. It does have one distinguishing characteristic."

"That being?"

"It's got a white streak or stripe on the side. This information came from Anna, the little girl, who saw it several times yesterday when she was unpacking. I'm thinking someone could have keyed it and when the grey was taken out, the white undercoat is what makes the line."

"I can call the body shops in town. Maybe whoever owned it took it to one of them to get a quote," Jake said.

"Good thinking. Now here's where you get to use your acting chops to play the charming man you are for the woman you were dating at the DMV."

"That could be a little harder," Jake said. "We didn't part on the best of terms."

"Well, see if you can make her think you made a mistake or whatever. The girl was able to get the last five letters and number off of the license plate which was a California plate. It was a black plate with yellow lettering. Could have been the old original style or a new one. Given that she didn't say the car looked really old, I'd go with the reissue. The last five of the plate in question are A73Y2."

"Let me guess. You want my friend to see if she can find a grey car that has a plate matching the last five."

"Yeah, what do you think?" Arthur asked.

"I don't know if that can be done, but she's kind of a computer genius, so if anyone can do it, she can. When do you the need this?"

"Yesterday would be too late."

"I get it. You want it ASAP. Right?" Jake asked.

"Right. Jake, don't panic. I know it might take a while, but I'm counting on you."

"Did I hear a raise being mentioned?" Jake asked.

"No, but that might be arranged. Talk to you later."

CHAPTER THIRTEEN

"Dani, I think we need to leave," Arthur said when he walked into the kitchen. We still have a lot of prep work to do. I'll start loading your SUV and my van. Actually, I'll get Matt to do it. He's the one who will be here with Anna and Briana until we get home. I just got a text from him, and he's at the gate. I gave him the code."

"Perfect. Anna and I made three Black Russian Bundt cakes. She was a huge help. Anyway, that takes care of dessert. The appetizers are in the freezer and they're labeled. We're serving a scoop of gourmet vanilla ice cream with the cake, so put it in those insulated freezer boxes you'll find in the pantry.

"Briana did the vegetable balls yesterday, and they're in the fridge. The steak is in there as well. We'll need the salad greens, and I've already made the dressing. There are several boxes of things over there to be packed. When you're finished, I'll take a last look in the pantry and the fridge to make sure we haven't forgotten something."

"Dani, since we're taking both of our cars, I'll follow

you."

"Okay, let me go upstairs, comb my hair, and get my chef's jacket and our aprons. Back in a minute."

"Arthur, could I go with you and Dani? I promise I'd just sit in a corner and not get in the way," Anna said.

"Absolutely not, sweetheart. We want you to rest for a few more days. I'm sure in a couple of weeks Dani would love for you to come with us, but for now you just stay with Briana and Matt. I saw you unpack a couple of games. I'll bet they'd love to play a game with you. And don't forget Killer and Kiku. They're going to need some attention."

"Okay. When do you think you'll be back here?"

"By the time we do the cleanup, I would imagine about 11:00, but I hope you'll be sound asleep by then."

"I will be, but would you do me a favor?"

"I'll try. What is it?"

"Whatever time you get home, would you and Dani come in and tell me that you're home? I'd feel better if you did."

"Now that I can definitely promise you," Arthur said as Matt walked in and started to load the boxes Dani had packed.

"I heard that," Dani said as she walked into the kitchen.

"And you could do me a favor. Would you feed the dogs their dinner? They eat about 5:00. Killer gets two cups of this kibble and can of tuna." She looked down at Anna conspiratorially. "He thinks he's a cat."

"That's silly," Anna said, laughing.

"May be, but he loves cat food. And Kiku gets ¼ cup of kibble and about two tablespoons of this canned food. I feed Killer in the kitchen and put Kiku's food in the laundry room. I've never had a problem with them trying to get each other's food, but I think it's probably smart to separate them when they eat."

"Okay, have a good dinner," Anna said as she skipped upstairs to get games to play.

"Arthur, give me a minute. I just want to do a walk-through of the fridge and the pantry, plus the desk in the kitchen where I have all my notes."

"Dani, as organized as you are, there won't be any problems. This will go off so smoothly, you'll have to turn away business."

"Wouldn't that be nice," she said. She walked out of the pantry and said, "It's a go. As they say in show business, break a leg!"

*****

The St. Regis Resort, located right on the ocean, was the number one luxury resort in the Santa Barbara area with prices to match. Every room was actually a suite with a jacuzzi and spa amenities in the marble and gold-plated bathrooms. Each suite looked out at the Channel Islands in the Pacific Ocean. Huge bouquets of fresh flowers were in each living room and bedroom along with a complementary bottle of wine from one of the finest, and most expensive, wineries in the region.

When guests wrote glowing reviews of it, one of the things they always mentioned was the attention to even the smallest of details. Nothing was spared for the guests of the St. Regis Resort.

Dani and Arthur pulled around to the back of the hotel where the event kitchen was located and saw one of the kitchen staff waiting for them with a two-wheel dolly.

"We'll probably need to make a couple of trips, but thanks for being here. Sure makes our work easier," Arthur said as he got out of his van.

Dani opened her door and walked around to the back of her SUV and looked at the boxes Matt and Arthur had loaded. While she was there, she looked down at her personalized license plate and grinned. No matter how many times she saw the word "DANI" on it, it never failed to please her.

"Dani, go on in the kitchen. I can take care of everything out here. Give me your keys, and I'll park our cars over there," Arthur said, motioning. "They have a special lot for the kitchen staff."

She handed him her keys. "Thanks, I am anxious to get this thing going." She walked into the kitchen and was met by the event manager, Betty. "Ms. Rosetti, I have arranged for four servers for you tonight, plus an additional two people who will be in the kitchen at your disposal to wash dishes, help you prep, whatever."

"Thanks, Betty. You went over everything with me when I was here last week, so I don't anticipate any problems, but is there a number where you can be reached if some unforeseen disaster occurs?"

"Certainly, here's my card. It has my cell number on it, and I have my phone with me at all times. I did a walk-through a few minutes ago, and I think everything is all ready for you."

"Thanks, I'm looking forward to this."

The next few hours were a blur of getting the appetizers ready, plating the salads, finishing the steaks which had been prepped earlier, cooking the vegetables, and getting all of the rest of the food ready as it was needed. It was a very carefully orchestrated event, and Dani had spent a lot of time working out when to put things in the oven, when to take things out of the refrigerator, giving instructions to the servers, and generally overseeing everything.

"Dani, what do you want me to do?" Arthur asked.

"Start by putting the garnishments I cut this morning on the appetizer trays. When you're finished with that you can prepare the Caprese salad plates. I've cut the tomatoes and the cheese, as well as taken the stems off the spinach. Use that as a base. The basil has been picked and is ready to go.

"Just before serving, swirl a little of the balsamic

reduction on them. I want you to use the square white salad plates. The play of color with red, white, green and the dark balsamic will pop against the white."

Every time the kitchen door opened Arthur checked to see who it was. He'd locked the door that led outside out of caution for Dani. He thought if someone was going to try and do something to her, this would be the perfect time, because there would be a lot of publicity.

The event they were catering was the annual dinner for a very prestigious wine group in Santa Barbara. The president had brought the wines and consulted with Dani on the menu, so that each course would have the perfect wine accompaniment for it.

The dinner went off flawlessly. Several times the servers told Dani that the guests kept talking about how unique and good the food was. The pièce de résistance was the Black Russian Bundt cake. Moist, dark, and with a hint of alcohol, it went perfectly with the dessert wine the president had chosen.

They heard the guests leaving, and after a few moments of quiet, the president of the wine group came into the kitchen.

"Ms. Rosetti, I just want to personally thank you for a fantastic dinner. Truly it was the best our group has ever had. A number of the guests said they would be calling you for upcoming events they want you to cater. I noticed your cards were very skillfully placed on a table near the exit. I'm sure you'll get a lot of business from this dinner."

"Thank you. My sous-chef, Arthur, and I enjoyed doing it. I hope you'll consider us for your group's next dinner."

"Are you kidding? If I didn't have you, there is no doubt in my mind that I'd be thrown out of office. Thanks again," he said as he left.

When he was gone, Dani turned to Arthur and said, "Unless you can think of something, I think we're ready to leave. We've packed the boxes up, and there's a whole lot fewer of them than when we came here a few hours ago."

"Agreed. We're good to go, Dani. Why don't you give me the keys to your car, and I'll bring it to the back door?"

"Ms. Rosetti, I'll get it," Hector, the young man who had been assisting them in the kitchen said. "You had everything so well organized, I don't feel like I earned my keep, because there was very little for me to do other than a few dishes."

"Thanks, that would be helpful. There are a few more things we need to get and we can do that while you're getting my car. It's the grey SUV with DANI on the license plate. She handed him the keys.

A few moments later she and Arthur heard a huge explosion that was so powerful it nearly knocked them off their feet.

CHAPTER FOURTEEN

"Oh, no," Dani yelled as the kitchen door blew in from the strength of the blast. At the sound of the explosion, Arthur had pulled Dani towards him and the back wall, the door narrowly missing them.

"Arthur, what was it?"

"I'm afraid it was a bomb, and I have a bad feeling it was meant for you. Stay here while I go outside.

People were running to the scene, and Arthur could hear the sound of sirens. Dani's SUV was a twisted pile of smoking metal, and tragically, Hector had been killed as well. When Arthur ran to what was left of the car, he saw parts of it strewn all around the parking lot. There was no point in having the paramedics come. It was too late for Hector.

Arthur rushed over to the first police car to arrive and told the officer he suspected it was a bombing. He told them who he was, who his client was, and why he was sure that the bomb had been intended for her. Whoever had done it had rightly assumed that the car with the personalized license plate was hers.

It wasn't the first time Arthur had dealt with the aftermath of a car bombing, and he'd carefully inspected the underside of her car just before they'd left her house. He knew someone had put the device underneath the car while they'd been inside cooking.

The event manager had been texted and as soon as she arrived, she walked up to Arthur and said, "Is Ms. Rosetti all right?"

"Yes. I told her to stay in the kitchen. I don't think she needs to see either her car or Hector looking like this. Unfortunately, the strength of the explosion blew the kitchen door off its hinges. Can you get someone out tonight to fix it?"

"Yes. I have a complete list of people to call when we have emergencies. It will be fixed within the next couple of hours. I'll stay until it is. I overheard you say that you think it was a bomb, and it was meant for Ms. Rosetti. Why?"

"I don't know exactly. Although I am Dani's sous-chef for her catering company, I'm also the head of a security company. Someone wants Dani dead. She had an attempt on her life yesterday, but I was hoping it was an isolated one. Obviously, it's not."

Just then a police detective walked up to Arthur. "Sir, I'm Detective Steiger. I'll be in charge of this investigation, and I'd like to talk to you and Ms. Rosetti."

"Certainly, Detective. Ms. Rosetti is in the kitchen. Let's go in there."

When he walked in, Arthur said, "Dani, this is Detective Steiger. He's in charge and wants to talk to us."

"Certainly, Detective. What would you like to know?"

"I'd like you to tell me what led up to this and what you know about it."

Arthur looked at her and said, "Dani, why don't you start with the poisoned candy from yesterday?"

Dani told the detective everything that had happened since she and Arthur had picked up Anna at the airport and concluded with hearing the explosion.

"Mr. Martinez, I'd like to hear your version," Detective Steiger said.

Arthur told him basically the same thing that Dani had. Dani was unaware that Arthur had checked her SUV for a bomb underneath it right before they'd left her house.

"Detective, I'm assuming you have a bomb squad unit that will be assessing what happened. And I presume that when Hector started the car, that was what triggered the bomb to go off. Would I be correct?" Arthur asked.

"Yes, the bomb squad unit just arrived and they're searching for evidence right now. I won't know precisely what happened until they finish their investigation, but I assume your analysis is a fair one. Why?"

"I'm sure that I'm not a target of whoever did this, but would you ask one of your men to check underneath my car? I could do it, but since bombs are their specialty, they'd probably spot something that I might miss."

"Of course. I assume your car is locked," Detective Steiger said.

"Yes. Unless someone had a key to get in my car, they'd have to place a bomb on it or under it. From what I understand, it's usually placed on the underneath part of a car. If they could check, I'd feel better when I got in the car. Here's the key to it."

"I'll be back in a moment," the detective said as he walked out the door and called over one of the bomb experts.

"Dani, how are you doing?"

"I'm okay. I just feel horrible about Hector. He was doing a favor for me. I'd like to pay for his funeral. Would you find out the information so I can?"

"Yes, and Dani I know I don't need to say this, but this was meant for you. Someone is very intent on doing away with you. I want you to be even more vigilant than usual. Will you promise me that?"

"Of course, but Arthur, I can't imagine who it could be. Did you have any luck with the phone calls you made this morning regarding the names I gave you last night? We were so busy today, I never had a chance to ask you."

"I'm about 99% sure it wasn't Robert Greenberg. He's been in New York since last Friday, and then he's going on to Italy. And he's going with his fiancée. Did you know he was engaged to be married?"

"No, I hadn't heard that. Any idea who she is?" Dani asked.

"No. I talked to his secretary and used a fake name. Didn't think she'd see any reason why I'd need to know that," Arthur said.

"I agree. What about the other two?"

"I haven't heard anything, and I turned off my phone during the dinner. By the time we get home it will be a little late for me to call, but I'll follow up first thing in the morning."

Detective Steiger walked back into the kitchen and said, "Looks like your car is fine, Mr. Martinez. No signs of tampering anywhere on it. Do you think whoever was responsible for Ms. Rosetti's car knows who you are or anything about you?"

"I have no idea, but I would be somewhat surprised if they did. When I do things like this, I do them as Dani's sous-chef. I don't think anyone would have reason to suspect that I own a security company. The only people who would be aware of that would be my staff and the nanny that was just hired to take care of Anna, the little girl Dani told you about earlier."

"Let me make a suggestion. Keep it that way. It would

help if they didn't know. Naturally, I'm going to have to make a full report of this. Ms. Rosetti, you'll be responsible for contacting your insurance company. I'll send you the preliminary report for your records. Is there anything else I can do for you?"

"You could wait until I start my engine, just to make sure nothing has been tampered with," Arthur said with a laugh.

"It's okay. My men checked the ignition as well. I find this case interesting, because I can see there's a lot more to it than just a car blown up by a bomb. Mr. Martinez, do me a favor and keep me in the loop. And if you need a little extra muscle, give me a call. Here's my card and I'll put my cell phone number on the back. Ms. Rosetti, here's one for you as well. If for some reason you need some police help, please give me a call."

"Why thank you," Dani said. "I really appreciate that."

Detective Steiger looked down at the floor and in a quiet voice said, "Do you think you appreciate it enough I could get your autograph for my wife? She's never missed one of your shows. As a matter of fact, she recorded all of them, and many is the night she's watching them when I walk in the house."

"Of course, I'd be happy to. What's her name?" Dani asked.

"Marcella. That's spelled M-A-R-C-E-L-L-A."

Dani took a piece of paper out of the notebook that was

on top of one of their boxes and wrote, "To Marcella. I hope my cooking has brought you some enjoyment." She signed her name and handed the piece of paper to Detective Steiger.

"Thank you, Ms. Rosetti. Believe me, this will make my wife's day. And I wasn't just talking. You call me if you need me."

"Thank you. I'll keep your number with me at all times," Dani said as he turned and walked out of the kitchen.

"Well, Arthur, I'm worn out physically and emotionally. What about you?"

"So am I."

Just then two policemen came into the kitchen. One of them said, "Detective Steiger told us you could probably use a couple of extra hands with those boxes. Where should we put them?"

"In the maroon van that's parked a couple of spaces down from where the bomb went off in the SUV. I'm not sure if it's open or not, so I'll walk out with you, and thank you. We're beat."

"I'm sure you are," one of the policemen said as they loaded the boxes into Arthur's van. "Need anything else?"

"No, thanks. There's just one more box, and I can get that. Thank you very much."

"No problem," the man said as the two of them walked

towards their police car.

Arthur went back into the kitchen. "Think that's it, Dani. I can get this last box. Do you want to have one more look around?"

"Yes, I've probably already checked more times than is healthy, but I don't want to have to come back here. The great memories of the dinner we did have been overshadowed by some rather unpleasant ones." She walked around and said, "It's good. Let's go home."

CHAPTER FIFTEEN

The ride back to Dani's home from the catering event was uneventful. They purposefully didn't discuss the bombing and talked about what had gone well and what they would change at the next event.

"Of course, if word gets out that cars get bombed at my catering events, that might put an early end to VIP Catering Services," Dani said. "And by the way, let's not say anything to Briana or Anna about this. I don't want to worry them."

"Consider it done. Here we are, and everything looks to be fine. I see Matt's car, and I arranged for one of my men to park down the street and watch your house. He has a clear view of the road in front of your house as well as the front of the house. As I mentioned before, I'm going to stay here at the house until we get the person or persons who are responsible for trying to kill you."

They unpacked the van and took the boxes into the kitchen where Briana and Matt were sitting, having a cup of coffee. Matt jumped up and helped with the boxes.

Dani looked at the coffee and then said, "Arthur, you can have coffee or join me in a glass of wine. I'm afraid coffee would keep me up all night. Can I interest you in either or something else?"

"Yes, I'll have a glass of wine," he said as he carried the boxes into the pantry. "You can sort through the boxes tomorrow, but I thought I'd get all evidence of how hard we worked tonight out of your sight."

He took the glass of wine she handed him and turned to Briana. "So, how was our little girl tonight? Everything go okay?"

"Yes, the three of us played games for a while, then she fed the dogs. I was talking to her about what to fix for dinner when she told me she'd helped you prepare the Black Russian Bundt cakes and how much fun it was. She also told me she'd never cooked before."

"That's what she told me, too," Dani said. "I figured if she was going to live in this house that cooking built, she better learn how to."

"I don't think you'll have to convince her. I mentioned that at the last place I worked the girls had a favorite make-ahead breakfast casserole that we used to fix quite often. She wanted to know more about it, and bottom line, your breakfast enchilada casserole is in the refrigerator, compliments of your niece, with a little help from me."

"Oh, Briana, that's great. Thanks. I'm sure she enjoyed it. I'm assuming the ingredients for it were here."

"Yes, all except the tortillas, but fortunately when I went shopping yesterday evening, I'd bought some, so that worked out perfectly. Now if you don't mind, I think it's time for me to retire to the guesthouse."

"Not a bit. You've put in a long day. I'll be here most of tomorrow, so take a little time and get acclimated. Have a good night."

"Thanks, Ms. Rosetti."

"Briana, from now on let's make it Dani. When someone says Ms. Rosetti, I always look around for my mother," she said with a laugh.

"I'll walk you to the guesthouse," Matt said. "Just want to make sure everything's okay."

"Thanks," Briana said. "See you tomorrow."

When they were gone, Dani looked at Arthur and said, "Are you thinking what I'm thinking?"

"And that would be?" he asked.

"I'd swear I saw a little glint in both of their eyes when they left here."

"And, so what? They're both adults, and I can sure vouch for Matt. He's been working with me for several years. I know he's single, but that's about all I know of his personal life," Arthur said.

"Yes, I suppose you're right, but I just hired Briana. I

don't want to lose her right away."

"Dani, I think you're jumping the gun here. Briana and Matt just met today. They were with Anna all afternoon and evening. I rather doubt that any hanky-panky took place."

"I'm not insinuating that it did. All I'm saying is that this seems a little fast," she said.

"Dani, we have enough to deal with at the moment. A niece, a possible murderer, a bomber, and who knows what else? Let me give you some advice. Let this play itself out on its own. Don't get involved."

"That's why you're my best friend," she said as she finished her wine. "While you wait for Matt, I want to go up and see Anna to make sure she's okay." She stood up and left the room.

A moment later Matt walked back into the kitchen. "So, you want to tell me what's up with Dani's car?" he said to Arthur.

"What do you mean?"

"I've known you for a long time, and you get a certain expression on your face when something has happened. Put that together with the fact that when you left, Dani drove her SUV and when you came back, both of you were in your van, and hers was nowhere to be seen."

"Well, I could tell you that she decided to trade it in for a new one, and she had to leave it with the dealer. Okay, I just hope that Briana didn't notice it was gone. Here's the deal," Arthur said as he related to Matt the events of the evening.

When he was finished, Matt sat back and said grimly, "What do you want me to do, Arthur?"

"I think I could use another pair of eyes and muscle here at the house. I'm concerned that someone could get to Anna as well. If I'm not available, and they need to go to the store or something, I'd like you to go with them. If Briana wonders why you're here more, just tell her that I'm just being extra-cautious. That's all she has to know."

"I've had worse gigs," he said with a grin.

"I've noticed," Arthur said sarcastically. "Why don't you come here around 8:00 in the morning, and we'll see what the day brings? I have several feelers out, and I expect to hear something fairly soon. Anyway, thanks for being here today, and I'll see you in the morning."

Arthur walked upstairs and heard voices coming from Anna's room, Anna's and Dani's. He walked into the room where Dani was sitting on the edge of the bed.

"Hello, ladies. Anna, isn't this a little late for you to be awake?" he said with a raised eyebrow.

"Remember? You promised you'd come and wake me up when you got home. Aunt Dani did."

"Yes, and that's exactly why I came in here before I went to my room. How was your afternoon and night?" he asked.

"It was great. I had so much fun. Briana and Matt and I all played games, and then Briana and I made breakfast for tomorrow. You know, I've really had quite a cooking day. First with you and the cake and then with Briana and the make-ahead breakfast. We have to eat it tomorrow morning, okay?"

"Absolutely," Dani said. "I'm really looking forward to having someone else do the cooking. And now I think it's time for you to go back to sleep. How did the dogs do?"

"Matt took them out before I went to bed, and then they came up to my room and went to sleep next to my bed. See, they're still asleep. Silly dogs."

"All right, Anna, it really is time for you to go back to sleep. Arthur and I are home, Matt's left, and Briana is in her house, so it's time to call it a night."

"Aunt Dani, can I ask you something?"

"Yes, of course. What is it?"

"I'm not going to have to leave here and go somewhere else, am I?"

"No, you're going to stay right here and live with me. Why do you ask?" Dani said.

"Well, I was wondering what would happen to me if you weren't here."

"Why would you wonder that?" Dani asked.

"Because of that candy I ate. I don't want anything to happen to you, because I like it here, and I want to stay here."

"Anna, nothing is going to happen to me. Somewhere there is a person who evidently doesn't like me, but Arthur is making sure that they're going to be caught, so you'll never have to worry about that again. Okay?"

"Okay. Good night," she said as she rolled over on her side and closed her eyes.

I have to find this person, Arthur thought. *Not only for Dani but for Anna. She's been through too much and that child will not go into some foster home as long as I'm alive. If nothing else, I'll take her myself.*

CHAPTER SIXTEEN

"Anna, this breakfast casserole is delicious, every bit as good as something I could make," Dani said the next morning as she, Arthur, Briana, and Anna ate at the kitchen table enjoying breakfast.

"I'm glad you like it. What do you think I should make next?" she asked.

"I haven't gotten that far. Let me think about it. Anna, I have a pretty free day. I know it's early, but is there something you'd like to do today? After all, this is your new home, as well as your new city. We could take a drive downtown, and I could show you the harbor and the Mission. We could even have lunch on State Street. They've got some great restaurants."

There was a knock on the door and then Matt let himself in. "Good morning, everyone. Anna, is that the breakfast casserole you and Briana made last night?"

"Yes. Would you like some, Matt? There's plenty for you."

"Why thank you, Anna. I'll just take you up on your offer," he said as he sat down at the kitchen table and joined them.

"Matt, Anna and Dani were making plans for their day and thinking about showing Anna some of the Santa Barbara sights. I really need to make some calls and do some work from here. I'd like you to go with them."

"Arthur, that's not necessary. I'm sure Matt has other things to do," Dani said.

"No, I'm totally free and at your disposal. How about if I drive, and you can point out the sights to Anna and tell me where and when to stop the car."

"Aunt Dani, I know all about the people who first lived in San Francisco. Who were the first people in Santa Barbara?" Anna asked.

"The Chumash Indians were the first people in the area, actually they lived from the Paso Robles area in Central California all the way to Malibu which is near Los Angeles. You've probably heard of Malibu, because a lot of the movie stars live there.

"The Santa Barbara Mission was founded in 1786 and was built to encourage members of the tribe to join the Catholic Church. It's quite beautiful. We'll go see it today."

"I'd like that. Does the ocean look the same here as is does in San Francisco?" Anna asked.

"I think you better see that for yourself. It doesn't have a big bridge like the Golden Gate Bridge. There aren't as many ships here in the ocean as there are in San Francisco, but I think more people come to Santa Barbara to go swimming in the ocean than they do in San Francisco."

"Can we go in the ocean today?"

"Absolutely not. It's still spring, and the water is way too cold." She heard a knock on the door and then Josie walked in.

She walked over to Anna and said, "You must be Anna. Welcome. I'm Josie, and I come here three days a week. I'm so glad that you'll be living here. This will force your aunt to work a little less, and that's a good thing," she said with a laugh.

"You're just in time, Josie. We finished breakfast and are heading up to get dressed for a tour of Santa Barbara. Anna, why don't you go ahead, and I'll be right behind you. I need to tell Josie what I'd like done today."

"Josie, I don't think you've met Matt. He works for Arthur. We've had a situation come up that I'm going to let Arthur brief you on while I get dressed. See you in a few minutes."

"What's going on, Arthur?" Josie asked.

"It looks like someone wants to put an early end to your employer's life," he said grimly, as he told her about the events of the last two days. "Do you have any thoughts on who it could be?"

"None. What do you want me to do?" she asked.

"Keep calm for Anna. Don't let anyone come onto the property even if it's a delivery truck. Just tell them to leave whatever it is next to the gate. You can say that you're in the middle of something and can't leave it. Until this person is caught, and he or she will be caught, I'm sleeping here at the house. Matt will be here during the day, and I have a couple of men stationed nearby. You're totally safe."

"Why do you think someone is doing this?"

"That, Josie, is the million-dollar question. I have calls in to several people and hope to know more later."

"Ready, Matt?" Dani asked as she and Anna came down the stairs a few minutes later. "I looked it up on the Internet and the Mission opens at 9:00, so we can start with it. I haven't been there in years, but it's really interesting. I think you'll enjoy it. The Chumash Indians were particularly known for their baskets, and although most of them are in private collections, the Mission has some. I remember them as being really beautiful."

"Have fun, ladies, oh, and Matt," Arthur said. "Anna, the front of the Mission is really something with its twin towers and big cross outside. When you look at the front of it, you can also see the Santa Ynez mountains in the background."

"Kind of like looking out the back windows of the house?"

"Yes, kind of like that. Matt take good care of them,"

Arthur said, and they both knew what that meant.

CHAPTER SEVENTEEN

"What in the devil happened last night?" the man on the phone said.

"Look man, it wasn't our fault," Stefano said. "How were we to know the broad wouldn't get in her SUV and instead some kid would? We hung around so we could make sure it blew up, and we were as surprised as you are. The bomb we put underneath was perfect. Just a lucky break on her part."

"Seems to me she's getting a lucky break on everything. What happened with the candy? That seemed like a slam dunk."

"Yeah, that's what we thought," Stefano said. "We drove back and forth on that road in front of her house several times and then put it in her mailbox. Don't know what happened after that. We went down the road a bit and parked the car behind a big tree so we wouldn't be seen."

"Yeah, so what did you see?"

"We saw an ambulance and a couple of cop cars come through the gate to her house. The ambulance left a couple of minutes later, siren and lights going. Figured we didn't get the job done, cuz' you know if they're dead, they don't waste their lights and siren. We stayed there for several hours, hoping to find out what happened. Never saw anything, so we left."

"Stefano, how did you and Mario know the broad didn't die at the hospital?"

"We didn't. We looked in the paper yesterday and tuned in the news channels, but didn't see anything about her dying. And she's such a celeb, figured she'd get a lot of press. We decided she must not have eaten the candy, and someone else probably did. That would explain why the ambulance came to the house.

"I'd seen something in the paper when we were getting ready to knock her off about her company, VIP Catering Services, doing the catering for some big swanky wine group. It was being held at that fancy resort on the ocean a little north of Santa Barbara, the St. Regis."

"Good for you for remembering."

"Yeah, thanks, that's what I thought, but that sure turned out to be a bust. I called the number for the event and asked if the event was still going to be held. The woman told me it was by invitation only. I said something about I'd seen an article in the newspaper about VIP Catering Services doing it, and she said everyone was really excited, because it was owned by the celebrity chef, Dani Rosetti, and she was personally going to cater it."

"Good thinking. So then what?"

"I knew what kind of a car, or I should say, SUV, she drove, because we'd been watching her for a while. I also knew she had a vanity license plate with the word DANI on it. Figured she'd be there early in the afternoon to get everything ready, so rather than follow her from her house…"

"Glad you didn't. That would have been too dangerous. And sooner or later she might have recognized your car."

"Yeah, and that's another story," Stefano said.

"What about it?" the nameless man asked.

"Somebody keyed it, and now I got a nice long white line on the passenger door."

"You probably need to get that fixed ASAP. That could be a tell."

"That's what I thought. I went to a body shop and got an estimate. I told them it was for my insurance company, like I even have insurance on that thing. I just wanted to know how much it was going to cost me."

"Anyway, when she and some guy were inside the resort kitchen, Mario and I put the bomb underneath her SUV and triggered it to the ignition. Super simple. Unfortunately, she had some kid get her car, and he had an early night-night. Mario and I figured it was time to get out of Dodge when that went sideways.

"We've never met, and I have no desire to meet either one of you. It's better that way, but I think I have a way that we can get this job done."

"I'm all ears, cuz' I'm fresh out of ideas," Stefano said.

"I was at the event last night. I never met Dani Rosetti, but the dinner was flawless and fabulous. Naturally, I left before all of the excitement, but here's what I'm thinking.

"There was a small table next to the exit with some mints in it and her business cards. I took one, as did several others. She really is good, and if it wasn't for this business of having to do away with her, I would have liked to have had her cater an event for me. And that's my plan."

"You're going to have her cater an event?" Stefano asked incredulously.

"No. I'm going to call her this afternoon and tell her that I was at the event last night, and it was wonderful. Then I'm going to say that I'm having an event at my home in Montecito this Saturday night and my caterer just called me and told me she has a family emergency and won't be able to do the event."

"I think I'm likin' this," Stefano said.

"I'll ask her to come to my home. My home is at the top of a hill, and there's a long private tree-lined driveway leading up to the gates. Very private. I will tell her to come at 3:30 this afternoon. I want you and Mario to hide behind the trees, and when she stops at the gate to call me on the intercom, you can finish the job you started."

"That should work. We'd never have to get out of the car. I've got a long-range military grade rifle, and it will be a piece of cake. How are you going to explain a dead woman in a car in your driveway?"

"Simple. The mailbox is by the gate. I'll just tell the police when I call them that I went to get the mail and found her dead in her car. What I need you to do is look in her car and see if there's a note with the phony name I'll give her and a time. If there is destroy it."

"Piece of cake. You'll call and let me know the time?"

"I will. Plan on around 3:30."

"You got it. I'll be glad to put this one to bed, and I sure can use the cash. Where are you going to put it this time?"

"I haven't decided yet. Produce the goods and then we'll decide when and where."

"Okay. Mario and I will be waiting for your call."

CHAPTER EIGHTEEN

"Good morning, Carla. Were you able to find out the information I talked to you about?" Arthur asked.

"Yes, sir. I talked to my sister-in-law a few moments ago. She was working yesterday and then she went to her son's soccer game, and her phone was turned off."

"Has she seen Lucia since Anna came to live with Dani?"

"She was there the day after I called Ms. Rosetti and spoke to Lucia. My sister-in-law, Cindi, said that in the morning she was very angry. She yelled at her for not cleaning the kitchen the way she wanted it done and a bunch of other things."

"Sounds like she's not a very nice person," Arthur said.

"And you'd be right about that, believe me. I don't know what Anna's father saw in her."

"Is she attractive?" Arthur asked. "I've never seen her or

a picture."

"Yes. If you didn't know her, you'd probably think she was attractive, but later, when you get to know her, she becomes ugly. Anyway, Cindi said that she got a phone call just after lunch and she completely changed into a happy person."

"Did Cindi say who the phone call was from or anything more about it?"

"Yes, it was from a man that Lucia knew. He asked her to go to Napa for a few days with him. She told Cindi that he had business there, and he was going to pick her up at 4:00 that afternoon."

"And did he?"

"Yes. She also told Cindi he was a very wealthy man and a much better catch than Bruno Rosetti. She said she didn't know why she'd even bothered with Bruno, when she could have this man."

"Did Cindi see him?"

"Yes and no. He rang the doorbell, and Lucia met him at the door with her suitcase. Cindi looked out the window as soon as they left the house and saw them get into a limousine."

"I see. So it seems that she went to Napa with him."

"That's what Cindi said. She only works for Lucia one day a week, so she won't see her again until next week.

Does that help you, Mr. Martinez?"

"Yes, very much. Thank you."

"Mr. Martinez, how is Anna doing?"

"I think quite well. She seems to be very happy here. Dani and one of my men are going to give Anna a tour of Santa Barbara this morning. They were going to the Santa Barbara Mission first and then show her the ocean. She seems to have made friends with the dogs. As a matter of fact, they're sleeping in her bedroom, and she's started cooking."

"With Dani?"

"Yes, Anna actually helped her bake some cakes for a catering event she was doing and then while she was gone, Anna and her nanny cooked a casserole for breakfast. I think we might have an aspiring chef on our hands."

"Good. I always felt guilty that her father wouldn't let her be in the kitchen. He didn't think it was seemly for a wealthy person to cook, because that's why someone got wealthy, so they could hire other people to do things for them."

"Carla, I don't know what to say to that, so I'll just leave it. Again, thanks for your help."

"Oh, Mr. Martinez, one more thing."

"Certainly. What is it?"

"How is she doing with Chester? Does she still take him everywhere with her?"

Arthur was quiet for a moment and then said, "I haven't seen Chester since the day she arrived. I said good night to her last night, and she was in bed with the dogs asleep next to her bed, but there was no sign of Chester. In fact, I don't remember seeing him anywhere in her room."

"That's a good thing. She begged her father for a dog, but he refused to get her one. He said they shed hair and were messy and they barked all the time. I remember her telling me once that if she couldn't have a dog, she'd have Chester. I'm assuming now that she has real dogs, she doesn't need Chester anymore."

"I'm not a psychologist, Carla, but it sure sounds plausible to me. Again, thanks for everything."

CHAPTER NINETEEN

"Martinez Security, how may I direct your call?"

"Hi, it's Arthur. I want to talk to Jake. Is he available?"

"For you, yes. He told me to hold his calls because he was working on something for you. I'll get him."

A moment later Jake's voice said, "Just the man I wanted to talk to. Heard there was a little excitement last night. Are you and Dani okay?"

"Yes, but only because of a quirk of fate," Arthur said.

"I've learned you gotta' believe in those. Dani was spared for a reason, and believe me, all of us here said a prayer of thanks this morning. From what we heard, it sure could have ended up a lot differently."

"That it could," Arthur responded, not even bothering to ask where Jake had gotten his information from. Several members of his security team were very close with the police, and he imagined Jake had heard about it from one of them. He may have even called one of them as soon as he heard something on the police scanner his team constantly monitored.

"I have some information for you that I think you'll be interested in," Jake said.

"That's why I'm calling. What have you found out?"

"I've done quite a bit of digging on Jocko Lucchese, and he definitely has Mafia connections. According to my sources his uncle is Lorenzo Lucchese. He moved to Santa Barbara several years ago from Chicago, and I understand that he and Jocko have a close relationship."

"Find out anything that would tie Jocko to the Mafia other than his uncle?" Arthur asked.

"No, evidently it's a close family, but Jocko never wanted to go that route. He's been a wannabe actor for several years and just recently landed a plum role on that new television hit, Life in the City. It's jumped to the top of the charts, and he's become an instant star, or so say they say in Hollywood after someone has been trying to get their foot in the door for forever."

"Get anything on his girlfriend, Talia Myers?" Arthur asked.

"Yes. As you know, she worked on Dani's show as her sous-chef. She has a very good reputation and is well-liked. She just doesn't have the star quality that Dani has. She and Jocko recently got married, and she's pregnant. Word is that she's given up her dream of having her own television food show and exchanged it to be the wife of a big television star and play the mommy role."

"Any idea where they're living?" Arthur asked.

"Yes, they recently bought a big house in the Hollywood Hills in Los Angeles. Guess he feels he can afford it given his new status as a TV star."

"Got an address for him? Not sure if I need it, but it might come in handy."

"Sure. Here it is," Jake said as he read it off to Arthur.

"You did well with Jocko. Got anything else for me?"

"Yes. I called all the body shops in the area. I've made a few friends over the years with some of the owners, and one of them told me he didn't get a car in with a white streak, but he said he'd ask around, and why didn't I meet him after work for a beer and maybe he'd have something for me."

"I told him I was probably going to work late and asked how long he planned on being there."

"He told me it was kind of his home away from home and he didn't usually leave until around 11:00 or so. I told him I'd join him if I could."

"Keep going, I'm all ears," Arthur said.

"I spent hours working on this stuff yesterday and I was whipped. After I heard you and Dani were okay, I went to the bar down the block for a tall, cool one. Figured I deserved it after all the trauma, and that's where I was supposed to meet my friend from the body shop."

"I know the bar," Arthur said. "Been there a time or two myself. It's kind of the go-to place for a lot of people. I don't think I've ever been in there when it hasn't been pretty much standing room only."

"And it was last night. Anyway, my friend was still there and I went over to his table. He was with a couple of guys who owned body shops. Like I said, I'd made a number of calls yesterday about the white streak, but no luck. Anyway, one of the body shop owners said he had a car come in a couple of days ago with a white stripe," Jake said.

"Did you know anything about the guy or the body shop?" Arthur asked.

"Nope. Never seen him before. Anyway, this body shop owner said this Italian guy came in with a grey car that had a white stripe on the passenger door. The guy examined it and was sure someone had taken a key and scraped a strip, which exposed the white primer paint underneath."

"Not an uncommon way to get back at someone," Arthur said. "Happens with regularity."

"True. The guy said he remembered it because the owner of the car was one of the rudest people he'd ever been around. He had another guy with him. The owner demanded that the guy stop what he was doing and give him an estimate. He said he needed it for insurance purposes and wanted it written down. The guy I talked to said he was pretty sure the owner couldn't afford insurance and was just trying to make it look like that."

"Did he write one up for him?" Arthur asked.

"Yes, he told me to call him this morning and he'd give me the information on the guy. He's pretty sure the guy used a phony name, but he was able to get the license number. I called my friend at the DMV who was having a devil of a time trying to match the first two letters or digits with the five I'd given her to come up with a match for a grey car."

"I assume you gave her the license plate number the body guy shop gave you."

"Sure did, and she came up with a match in only a couple of minutes. The car is registered to Stefano Conti. Unfortunately, that's as far as I could get. The address he gave to the DMV is phony. Likewise, there's nothing in social media, which has become pretty much the first place I always check, particularly on low-lifes, cuz' they need the strokes they can get there, and it also fits in with their desire to be anonymous.

"Checked all my other sources and nada. All I have right now is his name, a description, the car make, the license plate number, and the fact he was with another guy."

"Let's go back to Lorenzo Lucchese. This Stefano seems too far down the food chain to plan these things. Give me what you've got on Lorenzo."

"He lives in a gate-guarded mansion in Montecito. You

know those homes are some of the most expensive in the United States, and if it's on the top of its own hill, that puts it in an even more rarified atmosphere."

"Age, married, kids?" Arthur asked.

"He's sixty-four and has been married to a woman named Sophie for forty years. No children. There are a number of references to him in things relating to the Mafia, but he's never been arrested, so obviously he's never done time. He owns a number of car washes throughout California. When he lived in Chicago, he owned them there. He sold them when he moved here."

"That would fit. From what I've heard from some of my law enforcement friends, car washes employ a lot of ex-cons. That would make perfect sense for him to hire people who are either in the Mafia or helped the Mafia after they got out."

"Yes, it certainly makes sense that a Mafia man would use that as a cover. I've also heard that car washes are used for distributing drugs and receiving money. Obviously not the drive-through ones with the customer sitting in the car.

"Evidently when the cars are in the middle of the wash cycle, they have something they use so that water won't get in the trunk when they open it to get the money out and put the drugs in. Cinchy. Some guy pays for the carwash and just like everyone else when the car is driven out, he gets in it and drives off. Later on, he distributes the drugs in the trunk to whomever. Sweet little setup."

"I could assign a couple of men to a couple of the local

car washes, but I don't think that would turn up anything relating to Dani," Jake offered.

"No, that would be a waste. Does he belong to any clubs, play golf, take trips?" Arthur asked.

"Yes, he belongs to the Valley Club of Montecito. It's very exclusive, and it claims it's one of the top one hundred golf courses in the United States. I checked with the club, and he plays there at least three times a week."

"Good to know, but again, not going to help me with Dani."

"No, but you're getting a sense of the guy. He's also a member of the Wine and Dine Club, which is one of the most prestigious wine clubs in the United States. There's a buy-in fee of $10,000, and only the most prestigious wines are served. In fact, I learned that vintners throughout the world lobby the president of the club to have their wine served, so they can advertise that it was served at a Wine and Dine Club dinner. It's a real big deal."

"Okay, the picture I'm getting is of a lily-white country club guy with golf and wine hobbies. Anything else?" Arthur asked.

"Not that I could find. His wife is a beauty and has her clothes flown in from France. Everything else was sealed up. There is nothing that would possibly link him to the Mafia other than my inference that Mafia people often invest in car washes. Unfortunately, he's pretty squeaky-clean, as his nephew."

"Find any photos on him?"

"Just one, and it was from several years ago. He and his wife donated a large sum of money to the PAWS Chicago group. It's a pet adoption organization that's nationwide. They believe in no-kill facilities."

"Are you kidding me? A Mafia guy who donates to a no-kill animal group?" Arthur asked incredulously.

"No judgment, here, Boss. Just reporting what I find."

"Maybe his wife is the one involved in it. At least that would make sense. Any idea where they lived in Chicago?"

"Yes, knew you'd want to know, so I checked it out. They lived in The Loop area in a very expensive penthouse which overlooked the city and Lake Michigan. I took a quick look at Zillow to get some idea of what it was worth and it looked to me like it was around three million. Of course that didn't include furniture, art, and stuff like that."

"Guess those car washes pay pretty well. Of course, anybody who lives in Montecito is worth big bucks."

"Yeah, while I was at it, I looked up the prices of homes in Montecito. The average house, and this isn't one at the top of a hill, was going for over three-and-a-half million. I'd say the car wash business pays even better in Montecito than it did in Chicago."

"Agreed. So the bottom line is we have a Mafia man at the top of a hill in Montecito. We have an actor whose uncle is that man, and we have a guy with a white stripe on his car who is Italian. And no dots to connect them to one another."

"Well, you've got the family thing with Jocko and Lorenzo and family counts for a lot with Italians," Jake said.

"Yeah that's true, but this is all way too flimsy to take anywhere, and meanwhile, Dani is still out there with someone who wants to kill her. I really don't like this. Guess I need to sit with it for a while and see what I can come up with. Oh, and Jake, about that raise…"

"Yes, sir," Jake said hopefully.

"I think you can consider that a done deal. Thanks for doing a very nice job."

"Thank you, Boss. I'll keep after it and see what else I can come up with."

"Again, thanks."

CHAPTER TWENTY

"Santa Barbara Police Station. This is Officer Suzy Johnson. May I help you?"

"Suzy, my name is Arthur Martinez. The detective on a case I'm involved with is Detective Steiger. May I speak with him?"

"Let me see if he's in, sir," she said.

"This is Steiger, Arthur. How are you today? Have you had a delayed reaction to the events of last night?"

"No, not really. I'm working on this case and kind of wanted to let you know what I've discovered. It may not have anything to do with the bombing, but I think there's a nexus. Here's what one of my men found out."

Arthur spent the next few minutes relating the conversation he'd just had with Jake regarding Jocko, Lorenzo, and Stefano.

"It's all good information, Arthur, and I appreciate you

calling me because it may tie into the bombing, but so far I'm not coming up with much. There were no fingerprints which wasn't surprising given the explosion and fire that followed it. If there had been any, the fire destroyed them."

"I figured that was a longshot I wouldn't bet on," Arthur said. "I have another longshot thought. First of all, does one buy a bomb pre-made to put on a car?"

"If they are for sale, I've never seen them. All of the car bombs I've dealt with have been assembled with parts that are easily available on the Internet. I understand that it's pretty simple to construct one of these things, and they're certainly effective."

"I see. I know what to look for when I search in and under a vehicle for one, but having never made one, I'm wondering if the person who bought the parts for it could be traced," Arthur said. "I'm thinking if they could be, that sure would be a help to get a smidge of a smoking gun on one of these people."

"Arthur, it's been my experience that Mafia men like Lorenzo Lucchese would never get their hands dirty with something like this, or really anything. They have many people available who will do the dirty work for them. That's how they make their living.

"I really think you can count Lorenzo out of this. He may call the shots on something and be the brains behind it, but you'll never be able to pin anything on him."

"Yeah, you're probably right, Detective. And since people can easily get these things on the Internet, there's probably no point in talking to people who deal in explosives to see if I can match Stefano to it."

"Let me put it this way. If you were working for me, I'd tell you to spend your time doing something else. All people have to do is look at a number of different sites, figure out what's best for what they want to do, and buy the stuff. It's easy to get and very inexpensive."

"One other thing, Arthur. My men spent a lot of time last night interviewing everyone they could find at the St. Regis event center, and no one saw anything. I imagine the person who did it knew that Ms. Rosetti would be at the event center early to get everything ready."

"Which we did," Arthur said.

"Yes, and they also probably knew that things would be quiet during that time leading up to the actual dinner. There's an overflow parking lot for the resort guests behind the lot for the event center. My guess is that they watched for a chance when they wouldn't be noticed and then put it on the underside of the car," Detective Steiger said.

"I think I told you originally that two people were spotted in that car with the stripe that I told you about earlier. Do you assume that the second person was a lookout for the person who attached the bomb to the car?"

"Probably. Arthur, with all the new electronics that are available in the marketplace, people have really gotten clever. They text one another with what is going on, and it's not a big leap to think that the person under the car got a text from the other one telling him or her when it was safe to come out."

"I've been trying to recreate this in my mind while we've been talking. Based on what we think, the bomb would have been put on the car probably around 2:00 or 3:00 in the afternoon while we were working inside."

"I would agree with that," the detective said.

"Do you think they stayed around to see if the bomb was successful? And I wonder what they did or where they went when they found out the wrong person was killed."

"My sense is that they probably left and then came back when they thought the dinner was winding down. I'm sure they knew there would be some cleanup involved, and then you'd leave. I would guess they came back about 9:00 or so and parked in that same overflow lot.

"From there they could easily see Dani's SUV, and as soon as the young man got in it and the bomb went off, I'm sure they left. We didn't even try to find them in the parking lot, because of that. Where they went after that, who knows?"

"The thing that's really frustrating me is that I have no idea if these people in the car, who I am assuming are the ones trying to kill Dani, are working for someone else, or if they're working for themselves."

"Arthur, right now there's no way to know, and we won't know until someone is caught. The problem is keeping Ms. Rosetti safe until the person or people are caught. Are you with her now?"

"No, I'm at the house doing some work. She's with one of my men and Anna. Dani wanted to give Anna a tour of Santa Barbara."

"I'm sure that your man is well aware of how vigilant he needs to be," the detective said.

"Yes, he's very aware. He's been with me for a long time, and there's no one I'd feel better about guarding Dani and Anna than Matt. He would lay down his life for them."

"I sincerely hope that's a figure of speech and not a reality."

"So am I, Detective, so am I. Thanks for taking my call. I appreciate your input."

"Not a problem, and as I told you last night, feel free to call me anytime. You have my cell. Oh, and would you give Ms. Rosetti a message for me?"

"Certainly, what is it?" Arthur asked.

"Tell her my wife was thrilled with her autograph. She's having it framed, and she's going to hang it in the entry hallway. I scored with that. Barbara hates my job and is always after me to find something to do that's not so dangerous. This morning she actually sent me off to work with a smile and a kiss. Believe me, that's a first!"

"That will make Dani very happy. Thanks again, and I'm sure we'll be in touch."

Little did Arthur know it would only be a few hours

before he would need Detective Steiger's help.

CHAPTER TWENTY-ONE

"Well, Anna, what did you think of the Santa Barbara Mission?" Dani asked as she, Anna, and Matt walked to the car where one of Arthur's security men, Nico, who Matt had decided needed to go with them, was sitting waiting for them. Arthur hadn't wanted a repeat of last night with an unattended car in case Dani was being followed, so Nico stayed with the car while the three of them toured the Mission.

"I thought it was beautiful. The gardens, the church, everything. And the outside is beautiful. I can see why it was called the Queen of the Missions. I loved the twin bell towers, and I've never seen a kitchen from the 18th century. I thought it was interesting," Anna said with a happy smile on her face.

"Have you been to any of the other California Missions?" Matt asked.

"Yes. My class took a field trip to the Mission San Raphael. You know it's not too far from San Francisco. It was an all-day field trip. The mission was very pretty, but this one is far more beautiful."

"I've seen several of them throughout the state, and I'd have to agree with you. The Santa Barbara Mission is the most beautiful," Dani said.

"Aunt Dani, have you ever been to a church service at the Mission? I know we just walked through it and it was so beautiful, I would love to go to a service there."

"No, Anna, I haven't, but I've always wanted to. Why don't we go there soon?"

"Could we? I'd love that," she said as they got to the car.

"Hi, everyone," Nico said. "Anna, what did you think of the Mission?"

"I just loved it, and Aunt Dani said we could go to church there some Sunday."

"My family and I go to the 9:00 a.m. service on Sunday mornings. I think you'd enjoy it. It's a beautiful service, and I don't know why, but it makes me feel good to go to such an old church with all of its history."

"We'll let you know when we go so you can look for us," Dani said. "Now I'd like to drive down State street and then cross over the 101 Freeway and stop at the pier. I want Anna to get a sense of the city she'll be calling home."

As they drove down State Street, the main street in Santa Barbara, Dani pointed out different shops, Chaucer's bookstore, restaurants that she liked, the Paseo Nuevo shopping center, and ended her monologue by pointing to the ocean in front of them.

"Artists often bring their art here and exhibit their pieces on that stretch of grass you can see over there," Dani said as she motioned towards a long narrow stretch of parkland, wedged between the street and the beach. "On a warm sunny day, it's really fun to look at all the different kinds of art and the people, with the ocean as a backdrop. It's something I never get tired of doing. Do you like art, Anna?"

"Yes, but I don't know much about it. I'd like to take some art classes some time in school," Anna said. "And where am I going to go to school, Aunt Dani?"

"I've looked into some schools in the area, Anna, and there are several private schools that I think you'd like. Next week I thought we could tour them and come to a decision. If we wait much longer, I'm afraid they'll be closed for the summer.

"I also thought I'd get you a laptop computer of your own, so you can use it for school and whatever. You could look up the different schools on it and see which ones interest you. That way, we won't waste a lot of time. Now, we need to get serious about lunch.

"Nico, let's park near the pier. I'd like to eat lunch at Brophy Brothers, so Anna can get a sense of the area. And their clam chowder is the best around. Want me to get some for you?"

"Yes, thanks, and I agree, theirs is the best. Are you

going to have your palms read while you're on the pier?"

"I've never done that," Dani said. "Is it worthwhile?"

"If it's the same fortune teller that my wife had a few years ago, probably not. My wife doesn't work outside the home, has a French manicure weekly, and wears a big two-carat diamond ring she inherited from her mother. I tell you this because the fortune teller told her she could see that my wife did not do manual labor and led a good life."

Dani started laughing and said, "What did your wife say to her?"

"According to my wife, she said 'Duh, anyone could see that. You're a fraud.' And I do think that's what she said, because the woman followed my wife out of her shop and screamed at her in some language neither one of us understood."

Dani, Anna, and Matt laughed, then Dani said, "What happened then? Did she follow you down the pier?"

"For a little ways," Nico said. "I decided it was time to do a one-up, so I very casually turned around and pulled my sport coat back, so she could see my gun. That was all it took. She turned around and went right back to her shop."

"But she never offered to give your wife a refund, right?" Matt asked.

"No refund, but the story was so good it was worth the money," he said as he pulled into the parking lot. "Enjoy your lunch, and I'll see you in a little while."

An hour later Anna, Dani, and Matt walked out of the restaurant and over to where Nico was waiting for them. Dani was holding a sack in her hand.

"Here you go, Nico, fresh clam chowder. I hope you enjoy yours as much as we enjoyed ours, although we did supplement ours with some calamari. It was Anna's first time eating it, and she asked what it was. I said I wanted to wait to tell her until she told me whether or not she liked it."

"And did you like it, Anna?" Nico asked as he opened the trunk to put the clam chowder in it and secure it from spilling.

"I loved it. I could eat a whole meal just of that, but if Aunt Dani had told me it was squid, I never would have eaten it, but the squid was delicious. We also got some chocolate peanut butter cookies, and we saved one for you. They're really delicious. I even got the recipe from the chef. He was pretty excited to meet Aunt Dani."

"Thank you. I'm a cookie freak. Where to now, Ms. Rosetti?" Nico asked.

"I think we've tired Anna out enough for one day. She can go home and play with the dogs for a little while. I need to make some notes from last night's dinner, check my emails, and do some bookkeeping. So long answer to a short question, we're ready to be driven home, and I'm sure you're ready for your clam chowder."

"That I am."

CHAPTER TWENTY-TWO

"Well, Anna, what did you think of your new city?" Arthur asked as Anna, Matt, and Dani walked into the kitchen where he was working at the kitchen table.

"I like it. The Mission was beautiful and we had so much fun. I even ate squid," she said as she sat down on the floor to be closer to Killer and Kiku.

Kiku, in particular, had been dancing around Anna, begging to be picked up. Killer just looked around to make sure that Anna and Dani were okay. It was obvious that he'd picked up on the fact that protecting them was to be his mission in life.

"Glad you had a good time. Did Nico go back to the office?" Arthur asked.

"Yeah," Matt said. "He told me to tell you he had some things to do there, and since I was staying here, and you've got someone else down the street and you were here, he didn't think he was needed anymore."

"That's fine. I need to go into the office for a couple of hours, so I'd appreciate it if you'd stay here until I get back. Why don't you go down to the guesthouse and tell Briana that Anna's back?"

"Sure, happy to, Boss," he said with a grin. After he'd left, Arthur looked at Dani and winked. She returned it, both of them thinking there definitely was an attraction between Matt and Briana.

"And you, Dani, what's on your schedule for the rest of the day?" Arthur asked.

"I want to go in my office and spend a little time reassessing what I thought really worked at the dinner last night and what I thought could be improved on. I also need to do some paperwork and look at my emails."

"Dani, I know you weren't too crazy about it when I suggested that we get the app for our smart phones that lets each of us know where the other one is. I have to tell you that given everything that's happened," he glanced down at Anna, indicating he didn't want to go into details, "it really made me feel better today to be able to know where you were."

"Good. It if makes your stress levels go down, it's worth it," Dani said.

"Just keep your phone with you. I'm going to take off. I shouldn't be gone all that long," he said as he stood up. "When I get back, we can go over some of the information I learned today about our mutual friends." Again, he looked down at Anna, so Dani would know what he was talking about.

Anna continued to pet the dogs and play with them while Dani went into her office and spent some time looking at her emails. She knew what most of them were about, but one of them caught her attention.

The subject line read 'I'd like you to cater a dinner for me in Maui in June.' She opened it up and began to read.

Ms. Rosetti, I live primarily in Hong Kong, but I also have a large home in Maui. In June I will be hosting a dinner for some of the top business executives in the world to interest them in a product my company has designed. I have reserved suites for them at a nearby hotel I own, but I want to welcome them with a dinner party at my home to begin the three-day meeting.

My wife is a huge fan of your — yes, your show is broadcast even in Hong Kong — and insisted she would not attend the dinner if I didn't have you do the catering. Believe me when I say my wife has a lot of influence in our household!

I realize it is somewhat short notice, but I will pay you well for your time. I can send my personal plane to pick up you and any of your staff and fly you to Maui. Naturally, you will have your own suites at the hotel. I would want you to fly in at least a day before the dinner to make yourself comfortable with my kitchen and the environment.

You can send a grocery list and I will have my assistant see that all of the necessary items you require are ready for you. I sincerely hope that works for you. And please feel free to bring your family and indulge in a little vacation while you're in Maui.

143

I hope to hear from you soon.

Donald Chan

Dani read and reread the email, thinking what a wonderful opportunity it would be, not only business-wise, but personally. She couldn't imagine a more fun thing to do with Anna than take her to Hawaii. She decided to talk with Arthur about it and see what he thought.

The pilot who had flown Anna to Santa Barbara, Steve, had said that he'd make arrangements for the plane to be flown to the Santa Barbara airport, and Arthur was making the arrangements to have it permanently stored there.

Since Arthur was a pilot, he could fly them to Maui, and the plane was large enough that it would have no problem going that distance. And if a couple of those guests were pleased with what she did, she'd probably get some new bookings from them.

Dani idly wondered where they were all from and then decided that was enough daydreaming. It was time to do the bookwork and make some notes from last night.

An hour later, her cell phone rang. She looked at the screen and saw that it was an unknown number. "This is Dani Rosetti. How may I help you?"

"Ms. Rosetti, my name is John Donati. I know this is terribly short notice, but I have a real problem. I am having a dinner party for a number of people I do business with this coming Thursday. These are the presidents and general managers of well-known national corporations.

"My caterer, one I've used for years, has had a family emergency come up, and she needs to fly to New Hampshire immediately. Her aged father is in the hospital and not expected to live. Naturally, she will be unable to fulfill her obligation to me concerning the dinner which she was to prepare.

"I was at the Wine and Dinner Club event last night and happened to pick up one of your cards as I was leaving. I had no idea it would be so fortuitous. I picked it up because every course you served last night was outstanding.

"As you can well imagine, at the moment I am panicked, and my wife has told me in no uncertain language that she will not prepare the food for the event. I am desperately hoping that you will agree to do it, even on such short notice. The menu has been finalized and my housekeeper is planning to do the shopping tomorrow.

"Please tell me you can do this. I'll pay you double what you normally charge. I've never been in a situation like this, and given the status of my guests, it's not an event where I can do take-out pizza," he said with a laugh. "As I said, I will make it well worth your while."

Dani was quiet for a moment and then she said, "I believe I can accommodate you, Mr. Donati. I would like to meet you, see the kitchen where I will be cooking, and the area where I will be serving. When would you like to meet?"

"The sooner the better, Ms. Rosetti. I was hoping you were free this afternoon. Once I received the telephone call from my caterer, I left my office to come home and attend to it. If you could possibly come at 3:30, that would be wonderful."

"Give me just a moment to look at my appointment calendar," Dani said, knowing full well she had nothing on her calendar for the rest of day. She deliberately had planned it that way, so she'd have a chance to relax.

"Yes, Mr. Donati, that would be fine. Where in the area do you live?" she asked.

"I'm in the Montecito area. Just for your information, since my home is up on top of a hill and parking is rather limited, I will have valet parking at the dinner. Additionally, I don't know how many people you plan on bringing with you to staff the event, but my caterer told me she'd hired three people to work the event. One would help in the kitchen washing dishes, etc., and the other two would serve as waiters.

"Obviously, being in the Wine and Dinner Club, I am a wine connoisseur, so you don't need to worry about the wines. I've already chosen them based on the menu my caterer and I worked out."

"Good, I'll be bringing my sous-chef, but other than that, I can certainly use your caterer's staff. I would appreciate their contact information, so I can touch base with them before the event."

"Not a problem. I'll give you that this afternoon. Now let me give you directions to my home."

Dani took notes while he spoke and when he was

finished, she said, "I'm looking forward to this, Mr. Donati. Montecito is one of my favorite areas of Santa Barbara. I'll be there at 3:30 this afternoon."

"I'll see you then. Just press the button on the guard gate, and I'll open the gates for you so you can drive up to the house. Until then," he said and ended the call.

Dani looked at the bottom of her computer screen and saw that it was already 2:30. She worked for half-an-hour and then went into the kitchen where Briana and Matt were playing a game with Anna.

"I just received a call from a new client, and I'm going over there now. It's an emergency catering job. His caterer had a family emergency, and he's desperate. Time is of the essence. Tell Arthur I'll be back in a couple of hours.

"I know he'll be nervous about me doing this on my own, but I'll be fine. Anyway, I want to drive my new SUV that the auto dealer delivered while we were gone. It looks really great, and I can't wait to drive it."

Matt stood up and said, "Dani, Arthur will be furious if you go alone. I really think I should go with you."

"No, I'd rather you stayed here with Anna. Honest, I'll be fine. I'll be back before you know it."

CHAPTER TWENTY-THREE

"Hi everybody," Arthur said a few minutes later. "Where's Dani? Still in her office?"

"No, you just missed her. She had to leave suddenly. Said a new client was desperate because his caterer had to cancel on him, and he wanted to meet with Dani as soon as possible."

"Did she say where she was going?" Arthur asked, alarm bells going off in his head.

"No, she said she'd be back in a couple of hours. I tried to talk her out of going by herself. I told her I'd go with her, but she was adamant about me staying here with Anna."

"Where was she before she left?" Arthur asked.

"In her office," Briana said as Arthur ran down the hall to Dani's office. He saw that the computer was on, and a notepad was in front of it. A sheet of paper had been torn off of it, but he could faintly make out an address in

Montecito from the indentations on the paper. Below that were the words, "at the top of the hill."

He ran out of the office and yelled, "Killer." The dog came running, and as the two of them raced out the front door, he said to Matt, "Call the office and have Jake and one of the other guys meet me ASAP at this address." He gave Matt the address as he and Killer got in his van.

He drove with one hand and called Detective Steiger with the other. Fortunately, the detective picked it up immediately. "Arthur, is that you?"

"Yes. You told me to call you if I needed some help, and I think we have an emergency concerning Dani. A big one. I need you to meet me at this address in Montecito, but I have a bad feeling it's a set-up for Dani. Don't have time to tell you all of the details right now. I'm on my way with a guard dog, but don't use your siren or lights. There's something about a long driveway."

"Sounds too convenient," Detective Steiger said. "The guy we were talking about earlier lives on a hill in Montecito. I know because I drove out there. I was curious and wanted to scope the place out. I'll have a couple of my guys there as well. There's lots of trees we can use. Park your car on the far side of the road that opens up to the driveway. From there you can easily go from tree to tree."

"Will do, Detective. I have two guys of mine meeting me there. I'll tell them to do the same. See you soon and start praying that we aren't too late."

*****

I must be crazy, Dani thought. *Trying to fill in for a caterer on a couple of days' notice is not how I like to do things. Arthur teases me about being anal, and he just might be right. I like to be totally organized and have everything done in advance. This sure isn't my style. I hope I can wing it.*

As she was turning off of Highway 101 and going into the Montecito area, she saw a Starbucks on Coast Village Road. *Perfect*, she thought. *I'm a lot more tired than I realized, and I rather doubt I'd impress Mr. Donati by showing up and yawning. I definitely could use some caffeine.*

Dani parked her SUV, got out, and walked into the crowded coffee shop. There were several people in line ahead of her, and she worried that she might be a few minutes late to her meeting.

She decided she'd just explain to him that she was feeling tired and had stopped at Starbucks for some caffeine. He'd been at the event at the St. Regis the night before and probably had a sense of how hard she'd worked, given the courses that he'd said he'd enjoyed, so he shouldn't be surprised that she was tired.

As it turned out, it was a cup of coffee that would save her life.

CHAPTER TWENTY-FOUR

"Mario, there's the driveway the guy told me about. I'm gonna' park about a block down the road, and we can walk up the hill, staying in the trees. If we drive up there, Rosetti will spot our car, and with everything that's happened, it might spook her."

"You're the boss, Stefano, Mario said. "What's the plan? Do we just off her from a distance using that military sniper rifle of yours, or do we get up nice and personal?"

"Nice and personal. I'd thought about using my sniper rifle, but if we try to do it from a distance, there's always a chance she'll move or something. Then, who knows? She might even have a gun, and it could get messy."

"Yeah, I think you're right. I'm ready. Got my trusty Glock with me. You gonna' do it, or am I?"

"I've kinda' developed a liking for doing this. I'll handle the killing. While I'm doing that, you keep your eyes peeled and make sure something unwanted isn't around. Don't like surprises when I'm doing work like this."

"Totally understand, but look at it this way. Third time's always the charm, and this is our third time."

"No more talking. From now on just use your hands to talk. We're going to go up the left side of the driveway and I want to get as close to the guard gate as we can. The guy who called said he was giving the guard the afternoon off, so we should be the only ones around. Us and Ms. Rosetti."

He locked the door on his car and motioned for Mario to follow him as they began to make their way up the hill. The road they'd taken to come up the hill had been steep and they were almost at the top of it, the estate sitting at the end of the gently rising driveway.

Mario motioned for Stefano to come closer to him. When Stefano was next to him, he whispered, "What time is she supposed to be here?"

"The guy said at 3:30. I wanted to make sure we got here before she did. I just looked at my watch and it's 3:15. We're good." He gestured for Mario to follow him to the trees that were close to the gate, then he leaned over and whispered. "We'll stay here. She won't be able to see us from her car, and when she opens her car window to push the gate button, I'll walk over to her with my gun out. You back me up."

Arthur drove up the hill the voice on the GPS advised, and when he got to the top of it, he saw a grey car with a white stripe on the passenger door, and knew whoever it was that wanted to kill Dani was already there. He drove two hundred yards down the back side of the hill and parked his car.

As he opened the door for Killer and gave him the command to stay, Jake drove up, followed by Detective Steiger. The detective looked around, saw the grey car, and walked over to Arthur.

"I see our friends are already here. Does Dani know about the grey car and the stripe?"

"No, when I called Jake and had him check it out, and later told you, she wasn't around."

"Good, I was afraid she might get spooked if she knew about it and then saw it sitting right here. You said you have two more men coming."

"Yes, I do," Arthur said.

"Text them and tell them to park their car on the back side of the hill like we did and then slowly make their way through the trees to as close to the guard gate as they can get without alerting anyone they're nearby. I did the same with the two policemen I have coming."

"What's your plan, Detective?" Arthur asked.

"I haven't really thought it out. How good of a guard dog is he?" the detective said as he looked at Killer.

"Excellent, according to the trainer I bought him from. I've used the trainer over the years, and a couple of my men have dogs, but I've never used this particular dog for an offensive situation. I bought him to provide protection for Dani."

"I like using them. We'll go through the trees. I didn't hear a car, so I don't think Ms. Rosetti has arrived yet, but we're far enough down the hill that she won't be able to see us. We need to get as close to the guard gate as we can without the grey car people seeing us. Keep the dog with you, and if you feel you need to use him to attack, turn him loose," Detective Steiger said.

In a few minutes their backup personnel had arrived. Arthur and Detective Steiger motioned for their men to follow them, and they began walking up the hill through the trees that paralleled the driveway. When they got to the top and in position, Arthur looked at his watch. It read 3:30.

He wondered if he'd read the indentations on the paper wrong, because Dani was always on time. Everyone who had ever worked on her television show was well aware of how much she hated being late, and had little patience with anyone who was. He began to worry that maybe she'd already been passed through the gate and was now in the large house he could see at the top of the driveway.

He checked his app and saw that Dani was just driving up the hill. Arthur was just getting ready to tell Detective Steiger when he heard a car engine and then saw Dani's new SUV begin to come up the driveway. His heart was beating a mile a minute, and he was praying that his best friend, Dani, would make it through this and they'd be able to capture the killer or killers.

Dani stopped her SUV next to the guard gate and rolled

down her window. At that moment two men stepped out of the trees next to the guard gate and walked over to her car, guns drawn.

"Well, Ms. Rosetti, we finally meet. Hate to tell you this, but the third time is the charm," Stefano said. "You escaped the poisoned candy and instead of you being blown up, that dumb kid from the resort was, but you know something? Sometimes you just can't escape your destiny, and it looks like you're going to find that out right now." He lowered his gun and pointed it at Dani's head.

"Attack," Arthur shouted to Killer. The two would-be killers were momentarily startled when they heard Arthur shout. They turned and looked over in his direction, and that was all the time Killer needed. Arthur, Detective Steiger, and Killer were close enough to where the two men were standing that in three giant steps Killer had thrown himself at both men, knocking them down in the process and causing them to drop their guns.

Arthur, Detective Steiger, and the others swarmed around the two men who were quickly handcuffed, their guns picked up. "Stand down, Killer. Stand down," Arthur said, remembering the command the trainer had given him to release Killer from the attack mode.

Dani was looking at them in disbelief through her open car window. "Arthur, Detective Steiger, what's going on? Why are you here?"

Arthur walked over to her car door on shaky legs and said, "These two men were going to kill you, Dani, but you're safe now."

She looked at the two men and said, "I've never seen them before. Why would they try to kill me?"

Detective Steiger looked at her and said, "That's exactly what my men and I are going to find out."

He turned to Arthur and said, "I think you and Ms. Rosetti have had enough excitement in the last twenty-four hours. Why don't you drive her home, and the two of you can come to the station tomorrow? I'll take these two down there now and give you a call later on and let you know what happens."

"Arthur, what does all this mean? That I'm not going to be doing a catering event here? Was this all a set-up and those two men were responsible for the candy and the bomb explosion last night?"

"Dani, get out of the car and go around to the passenger side. I'll drive, and in answer to your questions, I don't know. We'll have to wait until Detective Steiger calls us.

"There's only one thing I have on my mind right now, and that's to get you home. You've been through too much the last few days. I'm afraid you might get some sort of delayed stress response, and I'd rather it hit you at home than when I'm driving.

"Killer, come. Good boy. Kennel," Arthur said, patting him on his head as he jumped into the back seat. "Okay, time to go home. Dani, it's over."

On the way to Dani's house, all Arthur could think about was who was behind the multiple attempts on Dani's life and why. What could possibly be the motive? He was certain that Detective Steiger would tell him the two men had no idea who had hired them.

The fact that the attempted murder had taken place at the home of a presumed Mafia member was just too coincidental. And he was certain that if the Mafia man was questioned, there would be no way he could be tied to any of the three attempts to kill Dani. He couldn't wait to hear what Detective Steiger had to say.

CHAPTER TWENTY-FIVE

"Everything okay?" Matt asked as Arthur, Killer, and Dani walked into the kitchen.

"Yes, but I think Dani and I could use a glass of wine about now. I'll tell you all about it later," Arthur said as he walked over to the wine cupboard.

"Dani, what's your pleasure?" he asked.

"There a nice Syrah in there from Washington. I'd like that. So, Anna, what wonderful games did the three of you play today?"

"Well, we played Scrabble. They're better at it than I am because they're older, and they know more words than I do," she responded. "But I'm going to get better. It was fun. I really liked it."

"I told you I was going to get you a laptop computer. You can get games on it, and Scrabble is one of the games you can get. As a matter of fact, sometimes I play it on my computer when I need a break from whatever I'm doing,"

Dani said as she accepted the glass of wine that Arthur handed her.

"And Arthur and Anna, I have some news."

"What's that?" Anna asked. "Is it good news?"

"I certainly hope you'll think so. I do. I received an email from a man who lives in Maui, Hawaii, and he wants me to cater an event for him. His wife is a fan of mine. They live in Hong Kong, but he said he has a big home on Maui. He's having a dinner for twenty people from all over the world, so it should be interesting."

"What did you tell him?" Arthur asked.

"I haven't answered the email yet. He said I could bring my family, and we could make a vacation of it while we're there. He'll put us up in a suite, pay me well, and fly us there."

"Us?" Anna asked.

"Us, if you and Arthur would like to come with me to Maui?"

"Seriously?" Anna asked. "You're not kidding me, are you?"

"Nope. I just need you and Arthur to say yes. I think we'd have a wonderful time. I haven't been there for several years," Dani said.

"I've never been there, and it's on my bucket list," Anna

said.

"Your bucket list?" Arthur asked. "Aren't you a little too young to have a bucket list, and how do you even know about them? I thought it was only old geezers like me who had them."

"Oh, Uncle Arthur, that's silly. Everyone has a bucket list. They might call it by something else, but it's the same thing. I saw the movie about it. I know what it is."

"Arthur, what do you think about going there?" Dani asked.

"I'd love to. Like you, I haven't been there in years. I do think we should take the plane that was your brother's. I can fly it with no problem. No sense in having your client send one for us, and that way we could fly to one of the other islands if we wanted to."

"From what you're both saying, I'll take that as a definite yes. Fortunately, it's next month, so Anna, you'll still be out of school. I'll email the client back tomorrow. I'm too tired tonight to do anything but sit here and decide what I want for dinner," Dani said. "What does everybody want?"

"Hold the thought," Arthur said. "I just got a call I need to take in your office. I'll be back in a few minutes."

*****

"Good evening, Detective. All the paperwork done?" Arthur asked.

"Yes, and it was pretty much like we thought it would be. The two men, Stefano Conti and Mario Garza, don't know who hired them. We did get them to admit to putting the poisoned candy in Ms. Rosetti's mailbox as well as to putting the bomb underneath her car.

"Actually, we got a lucky break on that one. An employee of the resort came forward and told the manager he'd seen the man who had put the bomb under the car as well as the man getting into his car afterward, a grey car with a white stripe on the passenger door."

"That was lucky."

"Yeah, sometimes that's the way it happens. Anyway, one of my detectives went to the resort, and the man made a positive identification of both Stefano and Mario. I'm really glad there was a witness, because I thought a good attorney might do something about their admission.

"They're under arrest and being charged with murder and attempted murder. I think they'll be gone for a long time. The one thing we weren't able to do was establish a link between Lucchese and them. There is simply nothing. We rang the gate guard bell, and there was no answer. He either wasn't there or he wasn't answering.

"And legally we don't have a leg to stand on. An attempted crime happened on his property. Does that mean he had something to do with it? Without any evidence, no. Sorry, Arthur, I was hoping that Santa would give us an early Christmas present, but it didn't happen."

"Detective, thank you so much. I really appreciate you

dropping whatever you were doing when I called today. I wasn't sure what I was getting into, but I was really afraid for Dani."

"As you should have been. I doubt you've had time to process this, but you do realize that without you, Ms. Rosetti would be dead."

"You're right. I haven't had time to process it. The only process I'm doing at the present time is drinking a glass of wine and hope that it will help the jitters I'm still getting."

The detective laughed and said, "If it's any consolation, I still get them. I think you need to worry when you don't get them anymore. One more thing, I'll need statements from you and Dani. Your men came to the station and gave theirs. What time would be convenient for you tomorrow?"

"I don't think Dani has anything on her schedule, but I do. Let's make it late afternoon. Say, 4:30?"

"That would be fine, Arthur. My man will be there then. And take a little time to pat yourself on the back for a job well done. If I have any friends who need some security work done, I'll be sending them to you. Your instincts about everything were right on."

"Thanks, Detective. Hope to see you again, but under different circumstances."

The detective laughed and said, "Who knows? Maybe I'll win the lottery and hire you and Ms. Rosetti to cater my wife's birthday. She'd probably like it better than the robe I got her for her last birthday."

"Just let us know when and where."

*****

"Lee, this is Arthur Martinez. Been a while," Arthur said to the head of security at a major Los Angeles television station.

"Arthur, it's good to hear from you, but since we haven't talked for a couple of years, I'm assuming that there's something I can help you with."

"Yes, there is. I need to talk to one of your television actors, Jocko Lucchese. Is there any way you can make that happen?"

"Major, when you saved my life in Afghanistan, I told you whenever you needed anything, to consider it done. It's been a few years, but we both know I wouldn't be here now if it wasn't for you. Consider it done."

"Would I be pushing my luck if I asked for it to be done tomorrow morning?" Arthur asked.

"No, as a matter of fact that would be a very good time. I'm looking at the board here, and I see that they start shooting his show at 8:00 tomorrow. What time did you have in mind?"

"Well, I'm going to be driving there from Santa Barbara, and traffic could be a bear. What about ten in the morning? I'll leave here early."

"Sounds good. Matter of fact they usually take a

morning break from 10:00 to 10:45. That would work well. Just come to the gate, and I'll give your name to the guard. Drive down to building six, it's the far one on the left. I'll be waiting by the door for you with your pass, so you won't have to go through reception."

"Thanks, Lee. See you tomorrow."

CHAPTER TWENTY-SIX

The traffic was fairly light for a weekday going from Santa Barbara to Los Angeles. It usually took about two hours, and today was no different. The television studio was located downtown. Arthur pulled up to the guard gate and gave his name. The guard checked it, raised the gate, and told Arthur how to get to building number six.

He parked his van and walked over to the door marked "Enter." Arthur knew most people idolized television and movie stars, but having worked at a television studio with Dani for several years, he'd lost his awe of them. Arthur had quickly found out they were no different from anyone else. They had their good points and their bad points, just like everyone else.

"Lee, it's good to see you again. You look great. I don't think you've aged a day since I last saw you."

"Thanks, Arthur, and I could say the same about you. Must be the business we're in."

"Yeah, it certainly doesn't seem to lend itself to just

sitting around, watching the soaps, drinking beer, and eating bon-bons, does it?" he responded.

"I took the liberty of telling Jocko that someone wanted to talk to him. I made it sound like it was someone with law enforcement, so you wouldn't get blown off by him. Actually, he's a pretty nice guy.

"He's in the room over there, the one with his name on it. Just knock on the door. When you're finished, you don't need to do anything. Just take off, and seriously, it really was good to see you."

"Thanks for doing this Lee. I appreciate it. One of these days I'll tell you all about it over a couple of beers. Matter of fact, I'll even buy."

"You're on," he said with a grin as he walked down the hall.

Arthur knocked on the door, and a moment later, a male voice said, "Come in."

He opened the door and walked into a luxurious suite befitting one of the stars of the show. "Hello, Mr. Lucchese, my name is Arthur Martinez. Thank you for seeing me. Here's my business card," he said as he handed it to Jocko.

Jocko looked at it for a moment and then said, "Do you mind telling me what this is about?"

"Not at all. I own a security company, and I have been the personal bodyguard for a woman named Dani Rosetti.

I'm sure you've heard of her. Your wife was her sous-chef on Dani's television show."

"Of course. I've met Dani. Again, I'm at a loss. What is this about?"

"Several days ago, an attempt was made on Dani's life via some poisonous candy that was delivered to her home. Luckily for her, someone else ate the candy and nearly died. It was quite clear that the candy was meant for Dani.

"The following evening Dani was catering an event at the St. Regis Resort in Santa Barbara. Her SUV was parked in the kitchen parking lot. When the event was over, a young man working in the kitchen volunteered to get her car, so she could pack it up. Unfortunately, the car had a bomb planted underneath it, and the young man was killed when the bomb exploded."

"I'm sorry, but I still fail to see what any of this has to do with me," Jocko said.

"Stay with me, Jocko. Late yesterday a man who lived on a hill in Montecito asked Dani to meet with him concerning an emergency catering event at his hilltop mansion. He told her his caterer had a family emergency and had to fly out of town. He said he was desperate and she agreed to go to the mansion."

Jocko took a sip of water and Arthur noticed that his face had paled under his makeup.

Arthur continued, "Funny thing, Jocko, the owner of the mansion where they were to meet has the same last name

167

as you, Lucchese. Fortunately, a Santa Barbara detective and I, along with some of our men and a guard dog, were able to stop two men from murdering Dani when she arrived at the gate leading to the mansion."

Arthur noticed that Jocko had unconsciously begun to exhibit one of the most classic signs that someone is nervous, blinking rapidly several times.

"Is any of this sounding familiar, Jocko?" Arthur asked. "The name Lucchese, a mansion high in the hills of Montecito, and I didn't mention that the man is thought to have ties to the Mafia. Of course with that name it wouldn't be hard to assume that someone did.

"And gee, when the police pressed the button at the guard gate, which the man who had talked to Dani had told her to do, so he could open the gates for her, guess what?"

"What?" Jocko asked, nervously blinking again.

"No one answered. Kind of interesting when a man tells someone he needs a caterer, tells her to come to a certain house and gives her explicit directions on how to get there and to press a button, and then two men jump out from behind some trees and try to kill her. Makes a person think there's more to the story.

"This is in addition to the other two attempts on her life. And gosh, a couple of other things. Turns out your wife wanted to get her own television show when Dani decided to quit, but the producer in charge of the shows refused to give her one.

"Talk is that she was very angry and jealous of Dani. You see what I'm saying here, Jocko? Let me spell it out, so we're both clear about it.

"Here we go. Your uncle is Lorenzo Lucchese. Your wife is jealous of Dani and hates her. Makes one wonder if you said something to your uncle about how your wife hated Dani, and you sure would like something to happen to her. Maybe kind of a belated wedding present.

"And then three attempts are made on her life, and an innocent man is killed. Oh, I forgot to tell you that the candy that was meant for Dani was instead eaten by her niece, and she almost died. I think I heard that your wife is pregnant. Figure you sure would hate that to happen to your child-to-be, right?"

"What do you want from me, Mr. Martinez?"

"I want you to talk to your uncle and tell him that he is being watched, and very much on the radar of the police. Tell him that his car washes are being looked into, and if there is even a hint that someone is trying to do something to Dani, he will be exposed."

"I will," Jocko said.

"Oh, and there's one other thing. Just to make sure you're persuasive with him, I'm going to make you a promise. That promise is if there is any indication your uncle didn't take you seriously, and something happens, your baby and your wife will never be safe, anywhere. Do we have an understanding, Jocko?"

"Yes, sir, we do. I'm a man of my word, and you have my word that there will be no more problems for Dani." He stood up and said, "If you'll excuse me, I need to make a phone call before my break is over, and I think you know what that phone call will be about."

"I think you've made a very wise decision, Jocko. Good luck on the show and congratulations on the baby." He walked over to the door and said, "I'm glad you're a sensible man."

"I am," Jocko said, as he took his phone out of his pocket.

*****

On the drive back to Santa Barbara, Arthur was elated. He knew that Jocko would call his uncle and tell him to leave Dani alone. He might even tell him what Arthur threatened.

He knew what he'd done could very easily result in him having his private investigator's license revoked, but he wasn't too worried. Jocko and Lorenzo had enough problems keeping the police from looking any closer at them.

I imagine this whole thing came about because Jocko mentioned to his uncle about how much Talia hated Dani and how she'd like something to happen to her. He probably told his uncle several months ago, before he'd become an instant star or even gotten married.

Lorenzo had probably taken his time setting it up and never told Jocko what he intended to do. Well, I know one thing. I can't tell anyone about the meeting I just had, certainly not Dani, and not even the detective. It will have to be my little secret, and I have no regrets about doing it. Dani doesn't need to live in fear anymore.

Done, finis, over. Next stop, Maui, he thought with a grin. *I am so ready!*

RECIPES

CAPRESE SALAD WITH BALSAMIC REDUCTION

Ingredients:
1 cup balsamic vinegar
¼ cup honey
3 large tomatoes, cut into ½" slices
1 8 oz. package of baby spinach, stems removed
¼ tsp. salt
½ cup fresh basil leaves, chopped (I roll the leaves up into a bundle and use scissors instead of chopping them. Seems easier to me.)
¼ cup extra-virgin olive oil

Directions:
Stir balsamic vinegar and honey together in a small saucepan and place over high heat. Bring to a boil, reduce heat to low, and simmer until the vinegar mixture has reduced to about 1/3 cup, approximately ten minutes. Set the mixture aside to cool.

Divide spinach between four plates. Evenly place

tomatoes on top. Sprinkle with salt. Drizzle olive oil and balsamic mixture over tomatoes and scatter basil on top. Serve and enjoy!

BLACK RUSSIAN BUNDT CAKE

Ingredients:
Cake:
1 box yellow cake mix without pudding in it
½ cup sugar
1 cup vegetable oil
1 pkg. instant chocolate pudding mix, 6 ½ oz. size
4 eggs
¼ cup vodka
¼ cup Kahlua
¾ cup water
Optional: ½ cup chopped pecans
Glaze:
½ cup powdered sugar
¼ cup Kahlua

Directions:
Cake:
Preheat oven to 350 degrees. In a large bowl mix all ingredients at low speed with a hand mixer for 2 minutes, then beat at medium speed for 4 minutes.

Pour ingredients into a greased and floured or sprayed Bundt pan. Bake in oven for 60-70 minutes. Remove from oven and let cool in pan for 10 minutes, then invert and slide onto a serving plate.

Glaze:

Combine glaze ingredients and have ready when cake comes out of the pan and onto the serving plate. Using a thin wooden dowel or other similar instrument, poke holes in top of cake. Wiggle the dowel around a little to enlarge the size of the hole.

Pour the glaze over the top of the cake and inside the center opening, being sure to pour extra glaze into the holes punched in the top, so it seeps down inside the cake. Dust with extra powdered sugar just before serving. Cake is so moist it will absorb the powdered sugar.

NOTE: Recipe provided to me courtesy of longtime reader, Helen Kerr. Thank you, Helen! As Helen said to me when she sent me this recipe, "Be prepared with extra copies of this recipe. You're going to need them when you serve it to family or guests!

BACON RANCH PASTA SALAD

Ingredients:
1 (12 oz.) pkg. tri-color rotini pasta
10 slices bacon
1 cup mayonnaise
1 (1 oz.) pkg. dry ranch salad dressing mix
2 tbsp. cider vinegar
¼ tsp. garlic powder
½ cup milk
1 large tomato, chopped
1 cup shredded sharp cheddar cheese
1 (3.8 oz.) can sliced black olives, drained

¼ red onion, chopped
1 bunch green onions, chopped
Chopped fresh parsley or basil, for garnish

Directions:

Cook pasta according to package directions. Drain, rinse under cold water, and drain again. Allow to completely cool (Best to hold in frig for several hours, covered).

Cook bacon in a skillet over medium-high heat until crisp. Drain on paper towels, then cut with scissors into ½" pieces and set aside.

Stir together mayonnaise, ranch dressing mix, vinegar, and garlic powder in a large bowl. Stir in ½ cup of milk until smooth. Add cooked pasta, bacon, tomato, cheese, olives, red onion, and green onion to the bowl. Toss to coat. Chill, covered, at least 1 hour.

If the salad seems dry after chilling, toss with additional milk as needed. Garnish with chopped parsley or basil just before serving.

CHOCOLATE PEANUT BUTTER COOKIES

Ingredients:
2 cans (16 oz. each) chocolate frosting (I use Duncan Hines.)
1 egg
1 cup chunky peanut butter
1 ½ cups all-purpose flour
2 tbsp. granulated sugar

Parchment paper

Directions:
Preheat oven to 375 degrees. Set aside 1 can plus 1/3 cup frosting. In a large bowl combine egg, peanut butter, and remaining frosting. Add flour and stir until blended.

Drop rounded teaspoonfuls of batter 2 inches apart on cookie sheets which have been covered with parchment paper. Flatten cookies with a fork dipped in sugar. Bake for 8 – 11 minutes. Remove to wire racks. Cool completely. Spread remaining frosting on cookies. Enjoy!

NEXT DAY BREAKFAST ENCHILADAS

Ingredients:
2 cups deli ham
½ cup green onions, diced
2 ½ cups shredded cheddar cheese
1 ¼ cups half-and-half
10 flour tortillas (8-inch)
4 large eggs
½ tsp. salt
1 tbsp. flour
Garnish: cilantro sprigs, salsa, sour cream
Nonstick cooking spray
Aluminum foil

Directions:
Coat a 9 x 13-inch baking dish with nonstick cooking spray. Mix together the ham, green onions, and 2 cups of the cheese in a medium bowl. Put ½ cup of the cheese

mixture onto each tortilla. Roll up and place seam side down in baking dish.

Whisk together the half-and-half, eggs, salt, and flour. Pour liquid over tortillas. Cover and refrigerate overnight.

In the morning, preheat oven to 350 degrees. Bake, covered with aluminum foil, for 35 minutes. Remove foil and sprinkle remaining ½ cup of cheese over enchiladas. Bake for 10 more minutes or until the tops are golden brown and the egg mixture is set.

Serve with salsa, sour cream, and/or cilantro sprigs. Serve and enjoy!

NOTE: This is a very forgiving recipe. Play with it, using different types of meat, cheese, and garnishes like sliced black olives.

LEAVE A REVIEW

I'd really appreciate it if you would take a few minutes and leave a review of Murder at the St. Regis.

Just go to the link below. Thank you so much, it means a lot to me ~ Dianne

Link: http://getbook.at/MATSR

Paperbacks & Ebooks for FREE

Go to www.dianneharman.com/freepaperback.html and get your FREE copies of Dianne's books and favorite recipes immediately by signing up for her newsletter.

Once you've signed up for her newsletter you're eligible to win three paperbacks. One lucky winner is picked every week. Hurry before the offer ends!

ABOUT THE AUTHOR

Dianne lives in Huntington Beach, California, with her husband, Tom, a former California State Senator, and her boxer dog, Kelly. Her passions are cooking, reading, and dogs, so whenever she has a little free time, you can either find her in the kitchen, playing with Kelly in the back yard, or curled up with the latest book she's reading. Her award winning books include:

Cedar Bay Cozy Mystery Series

Cedar Bay Cozy Mystery Series - Boxed Set

Liz Lucas Cozy Mystery Series

Liz Lucas Cozy Mystery Series - Boxed Set

High Desert Cozy Mystery Series

High Desert Cozy Mystery Series - Boxed Set

Northwest Cozy Mystery Series

Northwest Cozy Mystery Series - Boxed Set

Midwest Cozy Mystery Series

Midwest Cozy Mystery Series - Boxed Set

Cottonwood Springs Cozy Mysteries

Cottonwood Springs Cozy Mysteries - Boxed Set

Midlife Journey Series

Midlife Journey Series - Boxed Set

The Holly Lewis Mystery Series

Holly Lewis Mystery Series - Boxed Set

Miranda Riley Paranormal Cozy Mystery Series

Chef Dani Rosetti Cozy Mystery Series

Debut Cozy Mystery Series

A Cozy Cookbook Series

Coyote Series

Red Zero Series

Black Dot Series

My audio books can be found at
http://dianneharman.com/audiobooks.html

Newsletter

If you would like to be notified of her latest releases please go to www.dianneharman.com and sign up for her newsletter.

Website: www.dianneharman.com,
Blog: www.dianneharman.com/blog
Email: dianne@dianneharman.com

PUBLISHING 9/10/20

MURDER AT THE CARNIVAL

http://getbook.at/MATC

There's so much to see and do at a carnival!

There's the smell of carnival treats like funnel cakes and cotton candy.

Games that give you a chance to dunk the sheriff or win a stuffed teddy bear.

Don't forget the Ferris wheel ride.

And yes, there's that unpleasant business about the murdered man lying on the ground in the parking lot.

When Linc and Brigid agree to host a chili booth at the Summer Carnival, they never thought the day would end in discovering one of their B & B guests, the popular host of the online travel show, "Take Five," murdered in the parking lot.

But was Micha really all that popular? Someone, actually a lot of people, certainly didn't think so, and it's up to Brigid and Sheriff Davis to figure out which one them hated Micha enough to kill him.

And it never hurts to have a huge Newfoundland dog help you track down a murderer, particularly when they can't be found!

This is the 12th book in the Cottonwood Springs Cozy Mystery Series by a USA Today Bestselling Author and Amazon All-Star.

Open your smartphone, point and shoot at the QR code below. You will be taken to Amazon where you can pre-order 'Murder at the Carnival'.

(Download the QR code app onto your smartphone from the iTunes or Google Play store in order to read the QR code below.)